"They're coming back!"

The jerk of Ezra's head toward the edge of the glacier was unmistakable. "Keep going. If we reach the rocks, we'll be harder to see."

But as they neared the edge of the ice, the plane shifted course.

Taking Haley's hand, Ezra helped her down the icy edge of the glacier onto the water-slicked, loose rock making up the boulder field at the base of the ridge. When he stopped to remove the spiky cleats from his boots, Haley stood beside him, shielding her face from the pelting rain and staring at the plane as it slowly circled over the area just northeast of them.

"What's that pilot doing?" Ezra yelled over the whipping wind.

"I don't kn–" She broke off, her mouth falling open, as a dark figure climbed out onto the wing and launched into the open air. Then another, and another. Five in total. Her chest tightened, her worst fears confirmed as moss green parachutes exploded from their backs after the jumpers had cleared the plane.

Coming for *her*.

Kellie VanHorn is an award-winning author of inspirational romance and romantic suspense. She has college degrees in biology and nautical archaeology, but her sense of adventure is most satisfied by a great story. When not writing, Kellie can be found homeschooling her four children, camping, baking and gardening. She lives with her family in western Michigan.

Books by Kellie VanHorn

Love Inspired Suspense

Fatal Flashback
Buried Evidence
Hunted in the Wilderness

Visit the Author Profile page at LoveInspired.com.

HUNTED IN THE WILDERNESS

KELLIE VANHORN

LOVE INSPIRED SUSPENSE

INSPIRATIONAL ROMANCE

LOVE INSPIRED® SUSPENSE
INSPIRATIONAL ROMANCE

ISBN-13: 978-1-335-55513-7

Recycling programs for this product may not exist in your area.

Hunted in the Wilderness

Copyright © 2022 by Kellie VanHorn

For questions and comments about the quality of this book, please contact us at CustomerService@Harlequin.com.

Love Inspired
22 Adelaide St. West, 41st Floor
Toronto, Ontario M5H 4E3, Canada
www.LoveInspired.com

Printed in U.S.A.

For I am persuaded, that neither death, nor life, nor angels, nor principalities, nor powers, nor things present, nor things to come, nor height, nor depth, nor any other creature, shall be able to separate us from the love of God, which is in Christ Jesus our Lord.

—*Romans* 8:38–39

For Jason—
here's to the first twenty years of adventures together.
I love you.

And for the Calvin GEO department,
with special thanks to Renee Sparks and Jamie Skillen
for allowing me to pester them with research questions.
(All mistakes are, of course, my own.)

With gratitude to the amazing women who have
now helped me pull off three books worth reading—
my agent, Ali Herring; my editor, Dina Davis; and my
critique partners, Kerry Johnson and Michelle Keener.
I owe you so many batches of cookies.
And to my family—your support means the world to me.

ONE

Haley Whitcombe's breath came in sharp gasps as she pulled up to the hangar and slammed her car into Park. Light streaming from the wide-open doors created an illusion of safety in the dark predawn morning. She'd managed to cut through some side streets to shake the black car that'd been tailing her since she left her father's company, Whitcombe Aerotech, half an hour ago. But there was no guarantee they wouldn't pull in any second.

She snatched the digital SLR camera off the passenger seat and dashed inside the open hangar doors, her bare feet protesting the impact on cool concrete. Her family's mechanic, Walt Stines, waved from where he stood beside her Cessna Skyhawk, wrapping up the preflight check. *Thank you, God, for friends who are willing to help at 4:00 a.m.*

Without asking questions.

Though it cost her a couple of precious minutes, she dug through one of the beat-up lockers along the side wall and found the spare change of clothes she kept there. The flight time from Seattle to Spokane was short—just under forty minutes—but traveling in this expensive, tailored suit would be miserable. Besides, she'd left her pumps in the emergency stairwell of the office building.

A few minutes later, she emerged from the ladies' room wearing boots, an old pair of blue jeans, a black T-shirt and a black leather jacket to fend off the early-morning dampness. Not her usual sophisticated style, but significantly more comfortable and safer for the cockpit.

It was a given that the daughter of James Whitcombe and future CEO of his aeronautics company would earn her private pilot's license, so Haley had attended an aviation high school. After finishing an engineering degree in college, she'd gone directly to work for Whitcombe Aerotech. For more than a decade, flying had been her escape from the pressures of work and family expectations, but she'd never thought it would become a literal escape.

But after what had happened tonight… She swallowed, looping the camera strap over her neck and holding it close, trying hard to forget finding that security guard with a gaping hole in his forehead. The blood and bits of bone spattered across the office carpet, his gold name badge still gleaming in the dim lighting. How many times had she waved at him on her way into work?

Now he was dead, killed by one of her father's most trusted employees, Chris Collins. Or one of Chris's henchmen. All because the guard had been in the wrong place at the wrong time, assigned to patrol the building's tenth floor on the night when Chris decided to steal plans to their newest prototype jet engine.

Haley had been in the wrong place too—when she couldn't sleep, she'd gone into the office, even though it was the middle of the night. She'd found the guard dead in the hallway and the camera out on the conference table, surrounded by jet engine plans. When she'd overheard Chris talking to someone, she'd snatched the camera, hit record and hidden in the adjacent office with the door ajar. Only to record his plans to deliver the camera's files to his buyer *and* frame Haley for the crime. Economic espionage and murder. Payback for the fact her father had chosen her as future CEO rather than Chris.

Then Chris had noticed the camera was gone.

Like that guard, Haley would be dead if she hadn't escaped down the emergency stairs and made it into the parking garage. But she'd barely pulled out before the black sedan had come after her. The lighted hangar would be sure to draw the driver's attention if they'd managed to track her to the airstrip. There wasn't a moment to lose.

Walt Stines looked identical to every other time Haley saw him—carpenter pants, tool belt, flannel shirt, safety goggles propped up on his head. He jerked a thumb to her Cessna as Haley approached. "Plane's all ready. If you get going now before the storm rolls in, you'll easily have your three miles for VFR. Want me to file a flight plan?"

Outside the hangar doors, a gibbous moon lingered above the horizon, preparing to dip out of the way for the sun in the next few hours. It was a clear night, but to the west, thick clouds gathered along the Pacific coastline. Not the best flying conditions, perhaps, but she'd flown at night before. And the last thing she needed was to be easily trackable. Flight plans were optional at the altitude she'd be flying.

"No, thanks, Walt. This one needs to stay low-key." Haley offered a tight smile before walking once around the high-wing, single engine plane, briefly double-checking the structural integrity.

"You've got a full tank. Gonna tell me where you're heading?"

She silently debated for a second, then shook her head. "I can't. I'm sorry, but you'll have to trust me on this one."

In the distance, tires squealed. Had they found her already? Her throat tightened. "Walt, you'd better shut off the lights. And get out of here."

He frowned, deepening the wrinkles around his kind eyes. "Haley, are you in trouble?"

"I… Everything's going to be okay," she said briskly, years of experience helping her project the confidence she didn't feel. "I'll see you again soon. Now cut those lights."

She climbed into the cockpit and started the engine, then taxied out of the hangar. The loud thrumming and familiar smell of leather and oil offered a bit of solace after this upside-down night. Walt cut the lights behind her, but at the entrance to the airstrip, a set of headlights turned in through the open gate in the chain-link fence. As the car barreled closer, Haley raced for the runway, pushing the safety limits and breaking airport rules. At least no one else was out here. The control tower staff wouldn't even arrive until closer to dawn.

She turned the plane onto the runway, her breath coming out in a whoosh as the Cessna picked up speed. The car had stopped—its lights gleamed like twin beacons in the darkness. Hopefully they'd given up. She'd get into the air, and in less than an hour, she'd reach

Spokane and her father's lawyer. Ford Anderson would know what to do with this camera and the evidence it held.

He'd clear up this mess before her father even made it into the office for the day. Then she could call Dad, fill him in on Chris and what happened last night and feel confident knowing his faith in her wasn't in jeopardy. Going to the Seattle police would've been easier, but Chris had friends within the force. What if he threatened or paid someone off to confiscate her evidence? It wouldn't take much to make it inadmissible in court, and it was all she had.

Something pinged off the outside of the plane, sharp and hard, like hail in a storm. Were they shooting at her? Haley clenched her teeth, keeping her hands steady and a close eye on the instrument panel. The Cessna reached its target speed and she pulled back on the yoke, lifting the plane off the ground.

A final parting shot made the body of the small plane vibrate, but then she was up in the air, out of range and climbing toward safety. She banked away from foggy Puget Sound then high above the northern Seattle suburbs before completing her 180-degree turn to head east over Washington's rugged, wild interior toward Spokane. Fear washed out of her body in a wave, making her shoulders sag. *Please keep Walt safe too, Lord.* Overhead, stars twinkled in an ebony sky, but to the east, the faintest hint of light promised the day to come.

Every muscle went taut as she caught a glimpse of blinking lights out her right-hand window. Another aircraft was approaching from the south. Was it coincidence? Or had her pursuers called for backup as soon as she turned into the airport?

Haley gasped. The other plane was heading straight for her!

She angled northeast, heading off course, but the maneuver would give her the extra clearance to pass the other plane without cutting it close. Except the other plane changed its course too, following her. Gaining with each minute.

Her throat tightened. Before she could debate her next move, a bright flash flared from the approaching aircraft, briefly illuminating its cockpit windows against the night sky. Half a second later, a loud boom rippled through Haley's eardrums and her airplane shook in a sudden tremor.

The instrument panel flickered, the gauges spinning wildly, and the plane dipped precariously to one side. Sweat slicked her palms as she coaxed the Cessna back onto a level orientation. After twelve years of flying, she'd been in some dangerous midair situations before, but nothing like this.

Whatever they'd hit her with had done serious damage. She was losing altitude fast, her stomach in her throat as her mind scrambled through a mental list of local airstrips, but if she guessed her location correctly, she must be out over national forest by now. Maybe she could make it to Chelan.

Before she could course-correct, another burst of light flared from the chasing aircraft, followed a second later by a flash out her right window. The plane shuddered violently, rattling Haley's teeth and nearly throwing her hands off the yoke. The engine sputtered. *Please, God, not in the dark, in the middle of the wilderness.* Then it died.

Forget a runway. She was going down, now.

* * *

Ezra Dalton wasn't sure what had woken him up. Some unusual noise breaking the early-morning sounds of the subalpine meadow and the steady gurgle of Thunder Creek below? Or the faint hint of the coming day lightening the darkness in the east?

No, not that. It was some instinct pulling at his gut, insisting something was wrong. He unzipped the entrance to his lightweight backpacking tent and surveyed the sky, where a million stars still twinkled overhead. There, to the west, over the glacier field.

A dark shape blotted out the stars above the mountains, gliding silently closer to the earth. Red sparks flashed at the thing's tail, illuminating a ripped rudder and the high wings of a small Cessna. His chest tightened. Whoever was in that plane was about to crash.

God, have mercy. Please help them.

He watched, frozen in place, as the plane slipped behind the nearest ridge and out of sight. Wind rustled the grass, bringing the scent of summer wildflowers and a hint of rain. No boom. No fireball bursting up over the ridge.

The moment passed and Ezra snapped into action. With brisk, efficient movements, he pulled on cold-weather layers and packed up his gear, keeping his helmet, ice axes and line easily accessible—just in case the pilot had crash-landed on a glacier. The moon was setting, the sun still lingering beyond the reach of the horizon, so he secured a headlamp on top of his National Park Service ranger cap.

He made the call to dispatch as he set off up the ridge, notifying them of the potential crash. He'd radio the exact location once he found it, so they could send in a helicopter. Prayerfully for rescue, not for removal of remains. The dispatcher warned him the radar showed a storm coming in with heavy precipitation. Once the rain and thunderstorms arrived, the chopper would have to wait until the skies cleared, leaving him a window that probably wouldn't be enough time.

His legs burned as he pushed a hard pace up the ridge. Both the darkness and the fact he was off trail made the hiking more difficult. Good thing this wasn't his first time out on backcountry patrol. Instead, this season marked his third since he'd convinced the police chief at his precinct in Seattle to give him a five-month leave of absence to work as a wilderness ranger in North Cascades National Park.

Now it had become sort of an annual tradition. Take a pay cut, switch uniforms, escape the city and the memories. His hand drifted automatically to the picture he kept stowed in his uniform pocket, over his heart, but he pulled it back.

Now wasn't the time for nostalgia and might-have-beens. God knew what He was doing, even if Ezra would never understand.

High above, the loud whir of a plane engine broke through the chattering of the early-morning birds. He glanced up, scanning the sky, and found the dark shape to the south. Flying alone? Or was this plane searching for the first? Maybe they'd spot the wreckage and be able to call in the location. He pulled a high-powered flashlight from his belt and flashed an SOS signal. The pilot might not see it, but it didn't hurt to try.

By the time he crested the ridge, the coming dawn had turned the sky in the east to a soft, milky purple. Thunder Glacier spread out a few hundred feet below him, a field of white gleaming softly in the darkness with massive Boston Glacier and a string of jagged, rocky peaks in the background. On the eastern end of the glacier, closest to him, rested a dark object that could've been a boulder at first glance, but from the shape Ezra suspected it was his downed plane.

He offered a quick prayer of thanks that the pilot had chosen the closer glacier. Less ice to cross to get to the wreck. Hiking glaciers was dangerous work, thanks to the constantly shifting ice, which created deep crevasses. In winter, snowfall formed temporary bridges but also concealed the dangers. Now that it was late July, the glaciers at this elevation were mainly dry and free of snowfall, making them safer to traverse.

Maybe he should put "safer" in mental air quotes.

The dark patch on the snow slowly resolved itself into an airplane as he worked his way down the ridge. In the distance, a creaking groan proved the ice wasn't as stable as it looked, and the scent in the air shifted from rocky earth to the biting crispness of snow. Once he reached the edge of the ice field, he swapped out his hat for a helmet, then unhooked his ice axes, knotted a line securely around one of the handles and secured the other end to his waist. If the worst happened and he slipped, a properly planted ice ax would arrest his fall.

Years ago, when he joined a mountaineering group in Seattle, he'd been so terrified the first time they went glacier hiking. Now he knew better. Most of the time it wasn't nature that killed you, but the normal stuff, the things you took for granted, like taking your kid out for ice cream. Or going for a sunrise flight. He fisted his hand and glanced at the plane, maybe a hundred yards away on the ice.

The sky was brightening in the east, streaks of orange breaking into the twilight of dawn, but thunder crackled far off in the west. A sudden burst of wind whipped down from the higher elevations, carrying a chill that nipped at his cheeks. He didn't have much time, a fact the dispatcher confirmed when he called in the plane's location.

"Winds are too high in Marblemount for takeoff. Over," she said.

"Copy," Ezra said, his jacket snapping in the breeze. "I'm proceeding with the rescue unless conditions deteriorate, over."

She'd told him to call back with an update as soon as he had one, and they'd try to get the rescue chopper out as soon as they could.

He picked his way across the glacier as fast as safety would allow, offering a prayer of thanks that the early-morning temperatures were low enough to keep the ice crust solid. Between the distant rumbles of thunder and the intermittent gusts of wind, the sound of an engine high above reached his ears. Surely that pilot couldn't stay up there much longer.

The exterior of the wrecked plane looked bad—one of the wings was shredded, the rudder broken off—but the cockpit appeared intact. Ezra ducked beneath the remains of the wing as the first rays of morning light crested the ridge to the east, illuminating the snow in a blinding glow of hot pink and orange. A bit of blue sky tried to fight off the storm, but thick, dark clouds advanced like an army marching across the high mountain passes to the west.

The cockpit windows were fogged up—a good sign. Whoever was in there was still warm. Hopefully still breathing. He found the latch and pried the door open. The pilot, a woman, was buckled into her seat, her head tipped forward and face covered by a curtain of blond hair.

"Hey," he said, nudging her shoulder gently. "You awake?"

She stirred, tilting her head back to lean against the seat. Then groaned and opened her eyes. Bright blue, like twin sapphires. He blinked, taken aback at finding a beautiful woman in the cockpit instead of some grizzled bush pilot. In fact, she looked vaguely familiar. But now wasn't the time to gawk, not when her eyes were having a hard time focusing.

"Hey," he said again. "Can you look at me? Are you okay?"

She shuddered slightly, as if moving cost her some unspoken effort, but managed to meet his eyes. He held her gaze for a moment, then shifted from side to side, watching as she tracked the motion.

"Where…what…" Her mouth hung open a second and she turned to the instrument panel. Then she suddenly straightened. "I've got to get out of here before they find me."

"Before who finds you?" Ezra asked, concern pinching his insides. She must have a head injury. "Hey, stay calm. I'm here to help."

"No, I'm sorry, I—" She stopped short, flipped a couple of switches, which had no effect whatsoever on the dead instrument panel, then unbuckled herself, shaking her head.

"Are you injured?" he asked, but she swiveled in the seat and nearly shoved him out of the way before he could move aside as she climbed out of the open door. Okay…guess she *wasn't* injured.

Her blond hair swung around the shoulders of her black leather jacket as she inspected the torn wing of the plane, seemingly oblivious to the fact they were standing on a sheet of ice. Or that the wind was whipping around them much harder than it had been only a few minutes earlier.

Only when she slipped and Ezra darted out a hand to catch her before she wiped out, did she finally look at him. "I'll never be able to fly this out of here," she said, pressing fingertips to her temples. "Where are we? And who are *you*?"

"I'm a wilderness ranger. North Cascades National Park." He tapped the badge on his chest before remembering it was buried beneath his layers of cold-weather gear. "It's on the hat." Which he'd replaced with a helmet… "You'll have to trust me."

She squinted up at his headlamp, her face contorting into a grimace. Like he wasn't meeting her standards for a rescuer.

"Sorry." He flicked the lamp off. No need for it now anyway. "I'm Ezra Dalton. And you are…?"

"Haley Whitcombe." She ignored his offered hand and instead dug a phone out of her pocket, going so far as to hold it up over her head, as if the extra foot of clearance would somehow give her cell service. "Look, I don't mean to be rude, but I've got to get to the nearest airport. Or car rental. Or phone?"

Whitcombe. It took a minute to place the name, but then he remembered. She was that aerospace magnate's daughter, the one parading around Seattle to every social and charity event and gracing the cover of the "people" section of the newspaper every morning. A big city girl who'd dropped out of the sky into the middle of his pristine wilderness, looking for the easy way out and every service at her beck and call.

"Listen, Haley," he said, a bit more firmly than necessary. "You can't call your way out of this. You crashed in a national park. There's a storm coming, and we're out in the open on a glacier. Our first priority is to get to cover. You can worry about transportation later."

She looked at him again, her eyes narrowing as her gaze swept from his spiked, crampon-clad boots, past the fifty-pound pack and up to the headlamp still perched on his helmet. Over the nearest peaks to the west lightning zigzagged down in a brilliant streak, followed a few seconds later by a crackle of thunder. The noise snapped Haley out of whatever reverie she'd gotten lost in, and she gave him a tense nod.

"Fine."

He unhooked the end of his rope from his belt and held it out toward her. "We need to secure this around your waist." When she frowned instead of accepting the line, he added, "In case you hadn't noticed, you landed on a glacier. All it takes is one misstep and you could vanish into a thirty-foot crevasse."

At least the stubborn woman listened to reason. She pulled the rope around her waist and Ezra secured it into a knot snug against her stomach. Now she was tied to him, and he was tied to the ice ax. He gave her a quick set of instructions on what to do, but she was too busy staring at the sky to pay attention.

Finally, he asked, "What are you looking for?"

"Have you seen another plane?"

"Yeah, there was—" He cut off at her frown. "What's going on?"

Over the rumbles of thunder, the mechanical whir of the airplane sounded nearby, as if talking about it had called it back. Against the early-morning sunrise, the plane itself appeared in the east, sunshine reflecting off its windows like a glittering jewel.

Haley's face blanched. "We've got to get out of here."

That's what he'd just said. "Sure, of course." He tried to sound soothing, but…what on earth was going on? What was this woman doing out here? "I'll take the lead."

As he spoke, she reached back into the cockpit and retrieved something that she looped over her neck and shoulder. A camera. Huh.

The plane flew over the ridge Ezra had hiked earlier, heading straight for them despite the thunderstorm bearing down from the west. Larger than Haley's Cessna, this one could probably fit a dozen passengers. It was close enough now he could see the way its wings bobbled in the wind gusts. That pilot must be having quite a time trying to keep the plane steady. What fool would fly in this weather?

They'd only taken a dozen steps away from the wreck when something bright burst from the approaching plane.

"Get down!" Haley screamed. She threw herself to the ground, covering her head with her arms.

A high-pitched whir zipped through the air, followed immediately by a concussive *boom* that knocked Ezra to his back on the ice.

On Haley's other side, the wrecked plane burst into flame.

TWO

Haley squeezed her eyes shut, curling her body into a ball around the precious camera as her ride went up in flames. Praise God she'd gotten it out of the cockpit before they'd found her. Snow bit into her cheeks and hands, and the wind wove icy fingers into her hair and yanked. A storm was coming, her plane was gone and she was stranded in the middle of nowhere with a virtual stranger.

Not to mention her head was throbbing—probably the result of crash-landing and sitting unconscious for who knew how long.

The rope at her waist tightened, pulling against her ribs, as a dark lump to her other side scrambled to his feet. She was grateful a park ranger had come to help her, but…

Now he was in danger also. Her chest tightened.

He was so bundled up under hiking gear and winter clothing that she had no clue what he looked like or how old he was—only a glimpse of warm brown eyes within the hood of his red jacket. But at least he seemed capable, and with this rope around her waist, he had literally become a lifeline to get off this glacier alive.

"Hey." He reached a gloved hand out to her. "We've got to get to cover and off this glacier before the ice melts and shifts."

This time she took the offered hand. Her fingers were so stiff they could barely wrap around his glove, but he held tight as he hoisted her to her feet. She followed him gingerly across the icy surface of the glacier, slipping and nearly falling more than once.

The dark clouds that'd been dogging her steps from the west were nearly overhead, but in the clear sky to the east she could see the other plane sweeping into a wide turn. Like it was coming back for another attack.

She tugged frantically at the rope. The ranger—what was his name? Edgar?—was a good fifteen feet ahead of her by now, too far to yell and be heard over the swelling wind and thunder. But she had to try. "Hey! Edgar! The plane, they're—"

Her feet flew out from beneath her and Haley crashed backward, her tailbone crying out in protest. The camera danced wildly against her chest, but the strap kept it from skittering away across the ice.

The ranger stopped and Haley pointed frantically up at the sky. He turned to look where she gestured, then glanced at the surrounding landscape.

Tension knotted up her insides as she scrambled back to her feet. Where could they go? Even once they got off the snowfield, the ground was barren rock rising toward a ridge. Maybe there'd be tree cover on the other side, but the plane would get here long before they could reach it.

"Come on!" he yelled. The ice ax, with its deadly sharp point, gleamed in his hand. The noise around them kept ratcheting up in volume every minute, and now slanting rain pelted them in the face. "There's a crevasse up here with a shallow shelf. We can get out of sight."

That did *not* sound safe. But neither did facing another one of those antiaircraft missiles or whatever else that plane was packing.

The icy rift was narrow, maybe three feet across, and dropped to a shelf about seven or eight feet down. Haley stared over the side into the glowing blue gully, her stomach flipping.

The ranger embedded his ice ax into the hard edge, then used it to slip over the side himself before holding out his hands to her. "Come on. It's stable. I've got you."

She swallowed, glancing back up at the sky. The airplane was heading in their direction, a small dark speck in the east growing bigger every second. Soon the pilot would see them and they wouldn't have time to hide. No matter how much she hated the idea, she had to trust this stranger.

Cold ice burned her hands as she sat on the rim of the opening. Leaning forward, she placed her hands on the man's shoulders and slid into space. Strong hands wrapped around her waist, catching her securely and lowering her to the ground. For a brief second, she caught a full glimpse of his face beneath the helmet. Chocolate eyes, dark stubble across his chin, just a hint of a crook on the bridge of his nose, like it'd been broken once. Undeniably handsome.

He released her and she turned her gaze away, focusing on more important things like pressing against the icy wall to make herself as unnoticeable from the air as possible. Her heart was hammering from the situation, not him. She'd sworn off dating and relationships two years ago.

The wind had vanished, along with the rain, leaving her in a frozen, blue ice castle. She was chilled to the bone, the cold rain soaking through her jeans and drenching her hair.

A moment later, the ranger ducked down next to her, tugged the headlamp off his helmet and stuffed it into one of the many little side pockets of his huge pack. Carrying that thing around had to get heavy. Why was he out here, anyway? No gray hair amid that stubble, but he was clearly older than the college summer intern crowd or fresh graduates who usually worked as rangers.

"Ezra." His dark eyes found hers. Something glinted in them—amusement? Or maybe it was annoyance. "My name is Ezra, not Edgar. I don't write horror stories."

"Huh?"

"Edgar Allan Poe? *The Raven*?" He shook his head. "Never mind."

Right. She'd never been good with literature. All that emotion and interpretation, nothing like the safe predictability of math and science. Up above, thunder clapped closer than she'd heard it yet, and she flinched. Clearly, God had thrown "predictable" out the window for the moment. "Sorry. I'm a little preoccupied, I guess. Ezra."

He glanced between her and the sky, where dark gray clouds had chased away the blue overhead. "Like with whoever is up there trying to kill you?"

The heavy pattering of rain reached her ears before she felt the first drops. She clutched the camera tighter to her chest, tucking it beneath one side of her jacket, as frigid drops battered the back of her head. "Could we...not talk about that right now?"

As if in answer, a radio crackled at his belt and a woman's voice came on, rattling off some code Haley couldn't understand. But the next words were loud and clear. "Repeat, this is an all-park alert. Seattle PD has issued an APB on Haley Whitcombe—female, blonde, five feet, ten inches. Wanted for economic espionage and murder. Believed to have escaped the city by plane and crashed in the storm."

She flinched as Ezra's stunned gaze fixed on her. His hand dropped to his belt. Reaching for the radio?

Or a gun.

Her mouth went dry. "It's not what you think—"

The radio crackled again, cutting her off, and Ezra pulled it out.

"You get that, Ezra?" the dispatcher asked.

"Yeah." He frowned, conflict darting across his features. Like he hadn't decided yet whether to report her or hear her out.

Don't tell them. Haley shook her head, silently pleading. The icy crevasse seemed to press in on her, and she braced trembling fingers against the frigid wall. Her temples throbbed so badly it made her dizzy.

Ezra kept talking, saying something about the other plane into the radio. Or a helicopter, maybe? His lips moved but the words made no sense. And why was everything spinning? Stars flashed in the edge of her vision, and her skin felt clammy and hot all at the same time.

Ugh, she was going to be sick.

The plane engine roared overhead—or was it blood thundering in her ears? Before she could look up to check, her knees gave way and she was slipping, down, down, into senseless black.

"Ms. Whitcombe. Haley!" Ezra's voice came from far away, groping through the thick fog in her brain.

Cold rain pelted her face, but delicious warmth wrapped around her frozen fingers. She pried her heavy eyelids open.

"Haley?" His face hovered over hers, and she realized with a start that he held her head in his lap, rubbing her hands in his. Biting cold ripped through her back and legs from the icy ledge.

She turned her head then squeezed her eyes shut. The edge was right there, a foot away, and she'd roll into nothingness.

"Hey, stay with me."

"What…happened?" She forced herself to look at him.

"You blacked out." He lifted her hands, blowing on them, his breath like a little furnace bringing feeling back into her fingers.

"Between the crash, and the cold, and the explosion…" He shook his head, his lips pressed together. "It's a wonder you made it this far."

And the announcement from the dispatcher. She had no idea Chris would move so fast. An APB already? The last six hours had been a nightmare, one traumatic moment after another. And she still wasn't safe, not by a long shot.

"Did the plane come back?"

"Not yet. I'm going to check. But first, take these." He helped her sit up, then pressed his thick ski gloves into her hands. His hands would freeze, and yet he'd given this bit of comfort to a complete stranger. Worse, to someone wanted for murder. She *should* refuse them, but as he helped her slide her stiff fingers into the soft fleece lining, she couldn't resist the warmth.

Static crackled from the radio again as another clap of thunder boomed overhead, closer now. The small black unit lay on the ice behind Ezra—he must've dropped it when she fainted.

"Ezra, it'll be another few hours at least. Copy?" the dispatcher said.

As he reached for the radio, the same high-pitched whine they'd heard earlier zipped overhead, sending a jolt of terror skittering through Haley's system. Ezra's eyes locked with hers for a split second. Then he looped his arm through the dangling rope and threw himself over her, shielding her from the explosion they both knew was coming.

The boom that followed sounded different, deeper, than when it had struck the plane. A rumbling that built and shook in a great ripple until the ice beneath her seemed to sway. From under Ezra's arm, she watched in horror as the ice groaned and an entire section of their ledge broke away with a shattering crash, close enough his radio was swallowed up in the endless shifting ice.

She screamed, pressing a fisted glove into her mouth to contain the sound. *Please, God. Please.* The prayer ripped out more in form than words as she burrowed closer to the ice wall.

"Don't move," Ezra ordered, still crouching over her as the creaking and shifting slowly stopped. The crevasse grew silent except for the soft pattering of rain on ice. "I'm going to stand up, and then you are too, nice and slow."

"What about the plane?" Her voice squeaked like a

mouse, and she clapped her mouth shut. *No one* ever saw her this scared or vulnerable.

"If we don't get out of this icy tomb, the plane won't matter."

She didn't dare nod, or even wipe away the rain streaming down her cheeks. Slowly the jacket over her head lifted as he stood. "Now turn, carefully, until you're facing me."

As she twisted around on her bottom, the ice creaked deep beneath her. She froze, holding her breath, expecting the whole shelf to calve away any second.

"Keep going." Ezra's voice was calm and steady, something solid in the midst of the chaos, and she latched on to the strength he offered. "Now," he said once she was facing him, "give me your hand."

She held it up and he wrapped his fingers around her wrist above the puffy glove, his ice-cold fingertips sliding beneath her jacket cuff. Despite the cold, strength flowed through that hand. Courage. Protection. A flurry of nerves flittered through her stomach at the contact, but she ignored it. He was only doing this because it was his job.

Their eyes locked, and he nodded. "On three. One. Two. Three."

Gingerly she slid her feet beneath her as he tugged on her arm, the tendons straining in both his hands. She let out a whoosh of air as she made it solidly onto her feet—

With a sickening groan the ice behind her shifted.

The sound filled the air, overshadowing the rumbles of thunder overhead. Dread cascaded over her as the shelf behind her slid loose in a huge chunk, leaving her heels practically dangling over eternity. Panic clogged her throat. She was falling backward, losing her balance, going over the edge with it.

Ezra tugged her close until her face smashed against the heavy fabric of his jacket. "You've got to climb out. Now. The whole thing's gonna go."

Without waiting for a response, he swiveled away from the safety of the wall to push her closer, then loosened the rope around his arm to lace his fingers together near her foot. "Here."

She stepped onto his interlaced hands and scrabbled up onto the frozen edge of the crevasse as he lifted her. Then he hauled himself up using his other ice ax and the line attached to the embedded one. Rain ran in cold rivulets down her face, soaking her hair, and she swiped at her cheeks as she scanned the sky. No sign of the plane. Was it too much to hope that shot was a last, parting effort?

Ezra started for the boulder field and she picked her way carefully after him, arms wrapped across her midsection and teeth chattering. It might be summer, but up here, the wet and cold had soaked through her clothing clean down into her bones. They hadn't gone more than thirty feet before she stopped, tugging on the line that tied her to Ezra.

Despite how reckless it was flying in this weather, the plane was still up there. She pointed at the dark shape now swinging around, ready to make another pass. Even from here, she could see it bouncing on the shifting air currents.

"They're coming back!" she screamed over the wind when Ezra turned to look at her.

The hood of his jacket obscured his expression, but the jerk of his head toward the edge of the glacier was unmistakable. "Keep going. If we reach the rocks, we'll be harder to see."

Between her black jacket and his brightly colored gear, they were sitting ducks out on the snow. The rocks would be better than nothing.

But as they neared the edge of the ice, the plane shifted course, veering slightly east to where the sky wasn't as dark.

Taking her hand, Ezra helped her down the icy edge of the glacier onto the water-slicked, loose rock making up the boulder field at the base of the ridge. When he stopped to remove the spiky cleats from his boots, Haley stood beside him, shielding her face from the rain and staring at the plane as it slowly circled over the area just northeast of them, ascending in altitude with each turn.

"What's that pilot doing?" Ezra yelled over the whipping wind.

"I don't kn—" She broke off, her mouth falling open, as a dark figure climbed out onto the wing and launched into the open air. Then another, and another. Five in total. Her chest tightened, her worst fears confirmed as moss green parachutes exploded from their backs after the jumpers had cleared the plane.

Coming for *her*.

Ezra squinted at the tiny figures falling from the sky like toy army men with parachutes. What on earth had Haley gotten into? At least the weather had forced the plane to quit firing on them. For a minute there, he'd seriously thought that crevasse would be the end.

Behind them, thunder built in a rolling crackle that

reached a crescendo right at their backs, reminding him they had more immediate problems.

Survive the exploding airplane. Check. Avoid getting shot. Check. Get off the glacier alive. Check. But they were still horribly exposed on a slippery boulder field in the storm, and now there were men on the ground too.

"Come on," he hollered to Haley, "we've got to get under cover."

She nodded, arms tucked tight around her stomach, blond hair plastered in clumps against her cheeks. His heart went out to her—she had to be freezing, on top of the trauma from everything that had already happened. Somewhere in the last half hour, since he'd cradled her head in his lap and risked his own life to save hers in the crevasse, it had gotten harder to remember she was wanted by the police, not a lost, vulnerable woman in need of protection.

Frustration churned his gut at his own weakness. He couldn't afford a lapse of judgment, not out here. He had to remember who she was—Haley Whitcombe, wealthy socialite, murder suspect.

And yet instead of blurting her name out to the dispatcher when he'd had the chance, he'd bitten his tongue. Haley had looked so desperate, and the least he could do was hear her side of the story.

Then the radio fell into a crevasse.

His knuckles ached from the fist he'd made and he relaxed his hand. Nothing to be done about it now. The authorities would be able to sort out the mess soon enough once the rescue helicopter came to find them. As long as he kept her alive until then.

He led her back the way he'd come earlier that morning, frequently checking to make sure she wasn't slipping on the loose rock. At least she had boots on—that was something. As they approached the crest of the ridge, he hung close to a large rock on one side of the makeshift path. The heavy rainfall obscured his view into Thunder Basin, making it impossible to tell if the paratroopers had landed in the glacial valley below or farther east behind the opposite ridge.

Partway down the slope, he tugged Haley off to one side where an overhang offered protection from the driving rain and a boulder provided a windbreak. He half guided, half stuffed her into the corner between the boulder and the wall of the overhang, then dropped his pack. He untied the ropes from around their waists, swapped out his helmet for the NPS ballcap and secured the rest of the ice hiking gear.

After fishing out a small towel, a couple of protein bars and a spare bottle of water, he held the towel out to Haley. "Here."

She slipped off his gloves and frowned at the small square of neon orange fabric. "What is that?"

Just the reminder he needed of who she really was. Somebody who thought nothing was good enough for her.

"It's a towel. You know, the packable kind for camping?" He didn't bother trying to curb the sarcasm. "Sorry we don't have anything from the Hilton on hand."

Taking it between two fingers, she held it in front of her face for a moment. "It looks like it's meant for cleaning eyeglasses."

"Trust me, it's surprisingly absorbent."

She unfolded the towel and wiped her face. Then her neck. Then her hair, until she had to wring out the water. By the time she accepted the protein bar and bottle without complaint, Ezra noted with some satisfaction that the frown had vanished from her face. Point scored for the park ranger.

"Thank you," she said softly, staring down at the food in her hands.

For the snack? "No big deal," he said, blowing off the gratitude before he could read anything into it.

"No, for saving my life." Her big blue eyes met his, making his breath catch in a way that was very *not* appreciated. He hadn't so much as looked at another woman since Sarah, and he wasn't about to start with a wanted criminal.

"You're welcome." The words came out more gruffly than he intended. He diverted his gaze away from hers. She stood silent for a moment, hands clamped under her armpits, chin pulled down to her chest. Like she'd somehow grown smaller in the last minute. Something twisted inside his chest, but he shoved the feeling away. He kept hearing the dispatcher's words playing in his mind. *APB on Haley Whitcombe. Wanted for murder.*

Why would a woman like her, a wealthy heiress who had everything, commit corporate espionage? And murder? He hadn't processed many white-collar crimes working for the Seattle PD, but he knew corporate espionage meant stealing trade secrets to sell to a foreign government. Had she stolen from her own father's company? Who was coming for her—a double-crossed buyer?

And was she a threat now? He had a pair of cuffs in his belt—not something he normally needed in the backcountry, but you never knew when you'd run into a rowdy drunk who wouldn't comply. He eyed her again, sizing her up. She was tall for a woman, but her build was slim. Hiking the ridge would be near impossible if he cuffed her.

The steady downpour had diminished to a misty, light rain, and the darkest clouds now crackled and spurted lightning to the east. They'd be able to move soon.

"How do I get to a phone?" Her words cut across his thoughts, so seemingly clueless about their situation that anger sliced through his gut.

"Oh, there's a pay phone down the trail."

Her eyebrows lifted hopefully. "Really?"

"No, *not really.* Did you miss the part where you crashed on a glacier? Or where we nearly died in the crevasse because somebody fired missiles at us? How about the part where the radio fell and now we have no way to contact anybody?" He clenched his jaw, fighting to control his irritation. How could he expect someone as pampered as Haley to fully understand the danger they were in?

"I'm really sorry I dragged you into this, Ezra. Point me in the right direction, and I'll hike out of here alone. You don't have to worry about me."

The anger surged up, burning his esophagus, and he stuffed his hands into his pockets to keep from shaking her shoulders. The woman was impossible. "Are you serious? You wouldn't last half a day out here without the proper gear. Especially with those men after you. And I'm not about to release a wanted criminal into the park."

Her eyes glittered hard as gemstones for a moment, as if she were about to lash back at his angry tirade, but then she softened, shoulders drooping. "It's not what you think. I'm being framed."

"Right." Wasn't that the same thing every criminal

claimed? He pointed at the camera bulging under her jacket. "And what's that? Your proof? Or maybe it's got whatever you were stealing and trying to sell."

"It wasn't me stealing. That's what I'm trying to tell you." Exasperation leaked from her voice. "My father, James Whitcombe, picked me to replace him as CEO. But the guy who got passed over, the next highest exec, Chris Collins, is the one who stole the plans and killed that security guard."

Yeah, right. As if he could trust her. The Haley Whitcombe plastered all over the tabloids had acting down to a fine art. He'd seen her face in every checkout aisle for a month after she turned down her boyfriend's big screen proposal at a Mariners' baseball game a few years ago. A photographer had managed to catch one legit expression of shock, but in every appearance afterward she'd shown perfect composure. Like whatever had happened meant nothing.

"Look," she insisted, holding out the camera. "You can see the proof for yourself."

The camera clicked on with a little chirp and she navigated to playback mode, then started the video. A small conference room appeared on the display, its table strewn with large pieces of paper. He squinted, trying to identify what was on the sheets, but the picture trembled so much it was hard to tell on the small camera display.

"Sorry, my hands were shaking," she said softly. "And there's no sound on the camera's playback."

Her hands were shaking that badly? Compassion wrapped around his insides, melting his anger like snow in the July sun. "Where were you?"

"Hiding in the storage space between this room and

my dad's office." She jabbed at the screen as a man in a suit walked into the picture pressing a cell phone to his ear. "That's Chris. He's making arrangements with his contact. Then…" the man glanced up, his gaze going directly toward the camera "…he saw me."

The picture went wild, flashing from dark to the floor to walls. "You ran?"

"Yeah, to the stairwell, then down to the parking garage and my car. He stopped at the stairs, but a car came after me, so he must've called for help." She turned off the camera and the screen went black.

Ezra let out a low whistle. "And whoever is helping him has some serious resources."

"Exactly." Her blue gaze bored into him. "That's why I have to get to a phone so I can get this evidence to someone I trust."

Would it be enough to prove her innocence? Maybe if the file included Chris's conversation, like she seemed to think. Seattle PD would be able to zoom in on those papers on the table too. *If* he could get her out of here in one piece.

He pointed down the ridge. "The dispatcher said she'd send the chopper to a meadow right down there as soon as the storm lets up. We won't have long to wait." He extended his hand to help her up.

Her fingers were ice cold. An image of his wife, Sarah, flashed through his mind—how cold her hand had been by the time he'd made it to the scene of the accident. She'd already been gone for fifteen minutes. Too late to say goodbye. Their three-year-old daughter, Kaitlyn, had joined Sarah in heaven only a couple of hours later in the hospital. He clenched his teeth, swallowing down the memory like a chunk of ice choking him. Where had that come from? He was usually so good about keeping it all buried. Now certainly wasn't the time.

"Put those back on," he said gruffly, pointing at the gloves Haley held in her other hand.

The visibility was improving, and he could now see across the narrow valley to the opposite ridge as they headed down the trail. Park Creek Pass loomed like a wall two miles to the south. He half hoped to find a collection of parachutes tangled up in the trees somewhere, like a road sign indicating where the jumpers had landed, but there was nothing.

And no way of knowing where the men were now, or what kinds of weapons they were packing. Whatever they'd used from the plane, it'd made short work of Haley's Cessna. Prayerfully that other pilot had dropped the paratroopers too far east, and they'd be stuck wasting precious hours scrambling over the ridge to get down into this valley.

Leaving the barren, upper elevations of the ridge, he and Haley dropped into the subalpine meadow, an open expanse of wildflowers dotted with short fir trees and shrubs. Uneasiness tugged at his gut. There wasn't much here in the way of cover. Haley seemed to sense it too, shrinking closer to his back as they walked and accidentally kicking his heels.

"Sorry," she said for the tenth time. The word came out softly, but it still felt too loud, a lone human sound amid the quiet of mist-soaked nature.

He paused, turning to face her. "Don't worry about it." Despite his words, her face was lined with worry, her cheeks still wan beneath the flush of exercise.

"Where are we going?"

"Down the slope, that way." He pointed toward the hiker camp, where he'd slept the night before—basically an open patch of meadow with a backcountry pit toilet and a marker to designate it as an official NPS site. "Not far."

Behind them to the west, the clouds were starting to clear, revealing pockets of bright blue sky. Good for a chopper landing, bad for avoiding being seen.

By the time they reached the camp, the mist had cleared and the sun was shooting streaks of gold through the clouds down to the glaciers they'd just left. The chattering of small animals and birds had started up again, mixing with a low buzz of bugs and the ripple of wind across the meadow. Sounds that Ezra typically found comforting, but today they seemed to conceal something more sinister.

He gestured beyond the camp to a clump of scruffy evergreens that would provide more cover. Deeper into the valley, Thunder Creek's low rumble provided a bass accompaniment to the soft meadow sounds. "See those trees? We can wait for the helicopter there."

"How much longer?" Haley glanced between the trees and the sky, the movement quick and jerky. Was she nervous about the jumpers, or about the rescue headed their way?

"Shouldn't be long now that the storm's moving on."

At least, he desperately hoped so. Because if the helicopter didn't get here before those paratroopers, they were in serious trouble.

THREE

Haley weighed her options with each step closer to the trees, flexing her hands inside Ezra's thick gloves. Her fingers and toes had thawed out since they'd traipsed down that winding, treacherous path from the top of the ridge, and now that the rain was clearing, the air promised a hot summer day. She knew, deep down, she was exhausted, but the adrenaline coursing through her veins gave her enough of an edge to keep going.

The men with the guns were a problem. So was the whole lost in the wilderness thing. And being wanted for crimes she hadn't committed. Catching a ride with Ezra on his helicopter would solve the first two issues, but then she'd be stuck with the bigger one—being taken into police custody. Chris must've used his police connections to get an APB out on her so quickly. He'd already had the pieces in place to make everyone believe she was the one stealing from the company. Did her father think the worst about her too?

And if Chris had that kind of power—and the support of whoever had tried to kill her today—what was going to stop him from finding a way to get this camera back? While she was being held by the police, he or someone under his pay could easily swoop in and "accidentally" delete everything on the camera or steal the SD card. All it would take was one police officer willing to cheat the system for a friend. Or a bribe.

Her proof would be gone. She'd be looking at fifteen years in jail for the economic espionage alone, plus even longer for the murder. Her stomach twisted as an image of that security guard popped into her head, followed by a surge of anger. Nobody deserved to have their life stripped away like that. Chris needed to be brought to justice.

When they reached the trees, Ezra stopped, removed his pack and leaned against a trunk. "Should be anytime now."

Haley hesitated, gnawing at her lip. Standing around waiting for a helicopter to take her to the cops sounded like a bad idea.

He squinted at her. "What?"

"Is there another way I can get to a phone?"

"Sure, a two-day hike with insufficient supplies and paratroopers after you." He shook his head. "Haley, I don't get it. Are you afraid they'll find us while we're waiting? Because this is a whole lot safer than charging through the wilderness unprepared."

Her fingers wrapped around the cool metal and plastic of the camera, solid and reassuring. She'd already spilled the whole story. Maybe telling him her suspicions wasn't a risk. "I'm afraid to go to the police. If Chris and whoever he's working for have the power to frame me and send a special ops unit out here to hunt me down, what's going to stop him from getting his hands on this camera?"

"I work for the Seattle PD, you know. When I'm not out here for the summer."

Haley froze. Maybe Chris already had a way to get to her, through this not-really-a-park-ranger man she'd been trusting.

Ezra didn't seem to notice the way his pronouncement had shifted the ground beneath her feet. "There are a lot of good people who work for the department," he continued, "and we have protocols for handling evidence. I can help you."

She tightened her grip on the camera. Was this a ploy to get the evidence from her? Would he report back to Chris? Or secretly delete the memory card as soon as she fell asleep? She should've listened to her gut, not told him anything—

"I won't touch it." He tucked his hands behind his back. "Seriously, Haley, you can trust me. I'm trying to keep you alive, remember? We're on the same team."

Oh, how desperately she wanted to believe him. To not have to handle this mess by herself and instead let him get her to safety.

But had she learned nothing from that debacle with Xander? He'd been so charming, so thoughtful and considerate, when they first started dating after they met at a charity ball. She'd been so swept away she'd missed all the warning signs that he wasn't really in the relationship because of her, but for what he could get out of it—her money and fame. It was little things at first, like Xander begging her to go with him to public places she'd rather avoid. Or the paparazzi coincidentally showing up outside the private restaurant they'd booked. He acted like he understood she wanted to keep their relationship out of the celebrity gossip circles, but that jumbotron proposal had been a real eye-opener.

Along with the fact he'd moved right along to the next woman a month after Haley broke up with him.

If there was one thing she'd learned from that experience, it was how easily she could be duped by a man telling her what she wanted to hear. Some people had a good read on others, but when it came to men, Haley obviously didn't.

And right now, Ezra was telling her exactly what she wanted to hear.

No way could she get on that helicopter. She had to slip away somehow. There must be a trail around here if there was a campsite, and a trail would lead to a road. Eventually. She didn't have any cash, but her phone had half its power. She could hike out, hitch a ride and get to cell service.

Ezra had stayed glued to her side since they'd reached the meadow. Even now, she could feel him next to her, like a bundle of heat she couldn't quite ignore. And if he *was* honestly just trying to help, putting him in danger wasn't fair.

While he scanned their surroundings, she stole a quick glance at his pack and utility belt. He'd pulled the radio out of there earlier. He must have a gun too. Would he use it on her if she ran?

Not if she had a good excuse… With a flash of inspiration, she shifted her weight from one leg to the other. Then wiggled, just a bit. "Um, I need a potty break. After that water earlier?"

His brows pulled together slightly, and he glanced at the freestanding, fully exposed pit toilet at the campsite in the meadow.

She shook her head. "Nope. No way. Not where everyone can see me."

"Fine. But don't go far, just out of sight. And you've got to go on a rock, or else animals will dig up the vegetation for a salty treat."

Her nose crinkled. "Ugh, no need for details."

"Can you survive without toilet paper?"

"I'll manage." She offered him a fake smile and handed back his gloves. "Be right back."

She slipped through the trees, keeping the thickest undergrowth between her and Ezra. Not until his forest green NPS cap had disappeared did she stop to catch her bearings. More meadow on this side of the trees, but many of the shrubs were so tall she couldn't see over them. In the distance to her right, she could hear the steady roar of a stream. Maybe the path was down there. Farther away on her left, a soft rhythmic thumping beat its way through the air, making her chest go tight. The helicopter.

Ezra would call for her soon. Then come looking. She kept going, blindly, dodging around nettles and spiky evergreens and big rocks that appeared out of nowhere. There wasn't a moment to—

The sharp crackle of a stick breaking behind her stalled the breath in her lungs.

"Stop." A man stood fifteen feet away, his back to a big boulder. Taller and bulkier than Ezra, he was dressed in green camo pants and a jacket with a pack slung over his shoulder. But even scarier than the army apparel was the gun he aimed directly at her. "Don't scream, or I shoot. Got it?"

Haley froze, locking her arms around her midsection to protect the lumpy camera beneath her jacket as her brain scrambled to come up with a plan. Was he alone, or were there others nearby? "What do you want with me?"

The man ignored her, instead pulling out a radio. "I've got her. Quarter klick northwest. She's alone." In the distance, the steady beat of rotors drew closer. His gaze darted from Haley to the sky beyond her, where a dark speck moved like a giant locust. "Chopper's coming."

The radio crackled out a garbled response, which she wasn't sure was even in English. Russian, maybe?

"No," the man responded, "they can't see us. But if the ranger gets to them, they'll send a search party. You find him yet?"

A chill arced up her spine. Clearly Ezra *wasn't* involved in all this, and now she'd put his life in danger too. Why did it have to be so hard knowing who to trust?

A second indecipherable answer came through, and then the man clipped the radio back on his belt and advanced toward Haley. "Time for a walk."

She balled her shaking hands. How could she escape, let alone keep Ezra from harm?

The man crossed the distance between them long before she'd come up with even a half-decent plan. The only option was to play along and pray for some way out. He prodded her back with the gun barrel. It took all her self-control not to scream.

"Move," he ordered.

"Where are you taking me?" She tried to keep her voice from trembling.

"Boss says it's gotta look like an accident. Otherwise, people will get suspicious."

Chris *had* to be behind this, worried that he couldn't keep up the pretense of her guilt if she were found with bullet holes in her head.

"Then why were you shooting missiles at us on the glacier?" she asked.

"Easy enough to destroy the evidence and make that look like a fiery crash. Nobody saw except the ranger. But don't worry, we'll catch him soon too."

Behind her, the helicopter grew louder as it approached the open meadow to the west. She prayed Ezra would give up on her and run for it. No sense in them both dying.

Anger and regret twisted her insides. Maybe running away hadn't been the best move, but this situation didn't come with a lot of viable options. Any, in fact. The worst part, though, was knowing her father would be duped into believing she had betrayed him. Chris would be given her job, and her father would lose his daughter. She'd never get the chance to set the record straight.

Why does it have to happen this way, God? After how hard I've tried? The sense of failure nearly buckled her knees. Was God showing her that she'd failed Him too?

"Get moving," the man commanded, jabbing the gun into her back again. Somehow Haley forced her feet forward.

Where did that woman *go*?

Ezra scowled at the trees before whisper-shouting her name again. "Haley! Get back here!"

He wanted to yell for her—after all, she had to be close—but extra noise was the last thing they needed with those paratroopers on the loose.

Through the trees, where blue sky was visible above the meadow, the helicopter drew closer. It'd be in position in minutes.

No answering footsteps came from nearby. He'd have to go find her. After stuffing his cold-weather layers into his pack, he heaved it back up onto his shoulders. With a grimace, he headed through the evergreen thicket in the direction she'd gone.

Nowhere in sight. There was no way she could've gotten lost, not that fast. She must've run for it—an overconfident city girl who thought the wilderness was no big deal.

Sarah would never have hiked out alone like that. His heart twinged as he pictured her smile, her gentle manner, the way her brown hair curled softly around her ears. She'd been humble and sweet and sometimes a little anxious, especially about his trips with the adventure club. Pretty much the opposite of Haley, who was bold to the point of reckless and blazing her way through life like an inferno.

Why was he comparing her to Haley anyway?

He shook away the errant thoughts. A noise filtered through the tall aster and columbine on his left. He froze, listening. The low, deep rumble of a male voice reached his ears, followed by the racket of somebody tramping heavily through brush—heading toward Ezra, from the sound of it.

He ducked behind a nearby rock.

"This is far enough," the man said. "Now we wait for your ranger friend to come looking. If my associates don't find him first."

He had to be talking to Haley. Ezra's stomach sank.

They'd found her first, and he didn't have much time before more men showed up.

Quietly he worked his arms out of the pack and set it on the ground as he assessed his options. Trying to signal the chopper for backup was out of the question. This guy would grow impatient and shoot Haley, and whoever was watching the chopper might try to take it out too.

No, he had to make a move to rescue her. Now, before any more men showed up.

In the clearing the man's radio crackled. "We're in position," he said. "Close the net."

On silent feet Ezra crept to the left side of the big rock, where a bush provided extra cover. A dark head bobbed on the other side of the foliage. The man shifted into Ezra's line of sight. Cropped brown hair, camo fatigues and what looked a whole lot like an AK-47 screamed military. Or ex-military.

He couldn't see Haley, but she had to be there. How could he get a jump on the man without her getting hurt?

He couldn't just charge in—he'd need to sneak up, so he skirted back around the rock and dodged behind cover until he reached the other side of the clearing.

In a minute he could see them again through the leaves—the tall, hulk of a man had a hand clamped around Haley's arm. She stood in front of him, her back straight and chin up, a fierce expression on her face despite the gun pressed into her ribs. A sudden flash of admiration for her surged in Ezra's chest, catching him momentarily off guard.

Ignoring the unsettling feeling, he focused his attention on the problem at hand—how to incapacitate her captor before he could shoot. The wind, which had been gusting ever since the storm passed, created enough noise to help mask his approach. If he could worm his way forward a few more feet undetected, he'd be able to grab one of the man's ankles.

He'd have to leave his own gun holstered to keep his hands free. With a silent prayer, Ezra lay full-length on his stomach and army-crawled beneath the bushes. A final push brought his head and shoulders to the very edge of the cover. As quietly as he could, he reached for the man's closest boot.

Please let this work, God. He held his breath as his fingers neared the shiny leather. Then his hands clamped around the hard surface, fingers jammed against metal brackets and laces, and he yanked with every ounce of strength he could muster.

The man cried out, the sound so loud in the woods it may as well have been a fire alarm, but he came crashing down onto the ground in front of Ezra. In a blur of motion Haley leaped to the side, but Ezra's full attention focused on the AK-47 now lying just out of her captor's grasp.

The man kicked, sending the sole of his heavy boot slamming into Ezra's forearm, and he momentarily lost part of his grip on his adversary's leg. Yanking with the other hand, he lunged from beneath the bushes and threw himself onto the man's chest, swinging for his face. The punch fell short as his opponent rotated beneath him, and for a second Ezra thought he might get loose and grab the gun.

But in a blur of black and blue, Haley jumped forward and swiped the assault rifle off the ground. She backed away with it, keeping the muzzle up in the air and herself well out of their reach as he and the other man wrestled on the ground.

The man twisted again, nearly throwing him off, but Ezra landed a hard punch to his face. The momentary distraction was enough to allow Ezra to pull his gun, and he brought the heavy handle down with a sharp *thump* against the man's skull. Instantly he went limp.

Ezra sat back, sucking in a couple of quick breaths. Then he drew a pair of handcuffs out of his utility belt, cuffed the man's hands behind his back and rolled him beneath the brush. Hopefully he'd be out long enough his companions wouldn't notice him. Holstering his gun, Ezra climbed to his feet.

Haley stood a few feet away, her lower lip quivering ever so slightly, the big gun gripped so hard her knuckles were white.

"You okay?" he asked softly.

She nodded but her eyes were clouded with exhaustion and fear. A wave of compassion poured through his system.

But now wasn't the time to comfort—not with more men closing in. At least one of them was probably watching the chopper. He prayed nobody got off it to search for him and Haley, or they'd be in danger too.

Ezra retreated to the other side of the clearing and recovered his pack. He was still tugging it back into place by the time he returned to Haley's side. She held out the big gun like it was a rattlesnake ready to bite.

He took the gun, slipped the clunky safety back into place, then held it back out to her, offering the strap. "Sling this over a shoulder and wear it against your back."

Her nose curled up in a crinkle that would've been

cute if she wasn't causing him so much trouble. *Or* wanted by the cops. Though between her evidence and the men after her, he could safely say she was innocent.

"It's either the gun or my pack because I can't wear both. At least, not easily. Besides, the safety's on."

This time she reluctantly took the strap, draped it over her head and twisted the weapon around behind her back.

When he held out his hand, Haley let him wrap his fingers around hers and tug her forward. They'd flee north toward the trailhead, which meant keeping her alive out here for two full days.

The thumping of the helicopter sounded overhead, and he glanced up to see it through the trees. Good—the pilot was safe, at least. And he hadn't heard any other gunfire. Maybe there was a way to signal it—

A radio crackled. Close. Adrenaline ripped through his system like liquid fire, and he pulled on Haley's hand.

"We've got to run. Now!"

FOUR

I'm sorry for putting you in danger. For tangling you up in this mess.

The words hovered unspoken on Haley's tongue as she half stumbled, half ran through the thick undergrowth in front of Ezra. Just when she'd thought it might be too late, he'd shown up and rescued her. "Thank you" didn't seem like enough. The apology he deserved didn't seem like enough.

But she couldn't offer any of it right now, not with another one of those thugs bearing down on them, armed to the teeth. Maybe more than one. Was this how it felt to be a deer hunted down in the woods?

For a moment she almost wished they were safely up in the air on that helicopter. But then the camera banged reassuringly into her side, reminding her that a lifetime in jail, losing everything she'd worked so hard for, would never have been worth the trade-off.

They ran until her lungs burned and her legs ached. The heavy gun dug into her back with each step, and the strap, crisscrossed opposite the camera's, felt like it was going to saw her neck in half. Thick undergrowth clawed at her legs and arms, dangling pine branches scaped her face and roots reached up to trip her. Occasionally Ezra would grunt out a direction, "that way" or "veer right." As they left the meadow behind and descended deeper into the valley, the forest grew denser, and the sound of the gurgling stream was an ever-present accompaniment on their right.

Finally, after what felt like an eternity of fighting through spiky foliage, Ezra pulled up behind her. "Let's stop here a minute," he said, the words coming out between gasps. That backpack he was wearing had to be heavy. Sweat poured down the sides of his face.

"Okay." Haley put her hands on her hips, then massaged the stitch in her side with her fingers. "Do you think we lost him?"

He pulled off his hat to wipe his arm across his forehead, revealing a head of thick brown hair that stuck up at odd angles, then covered it again. He'd taken off his jacket earlier, and now he wore a gray NPS uniform shirt with the park service crest embroidered on one of the sleeves. His badge gleamed gold beneath the straps of his pack. "For the moment, at least. Long enough to catch our breath. We're looking at a two-day hike out of here, minimum."

Suddenly Ezra stiffened beside her. He held up a hand, as if to warn her to stay quiet, and slowly scanned the surrounding woods. Then Haley heard it too—a crackling sound coming from the trees toward the creek. Ezra gestured for her to follow as he ducked into a thicket a dozen feet from the route they'd been trailblazing.

Haley dropped to her hands and knees next to him, crouching low beneath the brush, and waited as the sounds grew louder. When Ezra's hand lowered to the gun in his belt, her chest tightened. Life suddenly felt so fragile, as if one moment, one mistake, could sweep them away into eternity. All the years she'd spent working so hard to please her father seemed meaningless in the face of the *what-ifs*. She offered a silent prayer for safety, darting a glance at Ezra, wondering if he was the praying type too. But his face was a mask of concentration, revealing nothing.

What kind of man was he? He was serious now, but something about his eyes, either the light that occasionally glinted in them, or maybe the creases peeking at the corners, suggested he liked to laugh. What had driven him out here into the wilderness for a chunk of every year? No ring on his left hand—he wasn't married. Why? The questions swirled in her head as if they were a form of self-defense, her brain's way of distracting her so she wouldn't panic. She hoped she'd live long enough to get the answers.

The crackling grew closer. Haley held her breath.

Ezra's mind whirred, listening to the approaching hiker like a death knell. *God, could You let it just be a cross-country hiker?*

No, scratch that. He didn't want anybody else to be in danger. Next to him, Haley was as still as an ice sculpture. He couldn't see much from behind the thick brush where they were hiding, but the sounds said enough.

Seconds later a dark shape moved on the other side of their hiding place. A soft, Russian-accented swear word drifted through the leaves as the man reached the area where they'd been standing only minutes earlier. Ezra's fingers grazed the handle of his gun. If the man had any tracking skills, he'd find them before long.

He glanced at Haley. She was trembling, her nearer hand balled into a fist so tight her knuckles were white. What mattered right now was making sure she stayed safe, and that this guy didn't get the chance to notify the rest of his team.

The dark shape was moving again. Was he leaving? *Please, God.* Ezra squinted through the brush, every nerve frozen in place until the moment action was required.

No. Something inside his chest deflated as the man turned back, coming closer again. Ezra's neon green pack was practically a flag marking their hiding place. He pressed a finger to his mouth, looking at Haley, and gestured for her to stay. Her blue eyes widened, and he thought for a moment she might argue, but instead she nodded.

Any movement was going to catch the man's attention, especially with this huge pack on his back. Better to take the direct approach. Ezra shifted his weight silently off his knees onto his feet. Then he drew his gun and stood.

The man's back was visible, a blur of camo against the forest backdrop, as he stooped over searching the ground for their trail. He straightened at the noise Ezra made, but Ezra already had his handgun locked on the man's chest. Before the man could raise his AK-47 into position, Ezra called, "Freeze. Drop the gun and put your hands on your head."

The man assessed him for a long moment, eyeing his NPS ballcap and the gun in his hand, as if debating whether Ezra's aim would be true. But they only stood a dozen feet apart, so the man dropped the weapon and raised his hands.

"I'm going to walk around these bushes to you," Ezra said, "and you're going to kick that gun over to me. Got it?"

A muscle tensed in the man's thick jaw, but he nodded.

Ezra worked his way carefully around the bushes until he faced the man. "Now kick it over, nice and slow."

The man complied, nudging the gun closer with the toe of his boot until Ezra could slide it out of reach.

"Face down on the ground, arms out to the side where I can see them," he ordered. His adversary's jaw muscle twitched but he did as he was told. Now for the hard part—securing him without cuffs. Alone. With a size disadvantage.

He warily stepped nearer, nerves firing faster than a semiautomatic. When he was close enough, he reached for the man's left hand, twisting it up and around behind his back. One hand was now secure, but to get the other *and* the climbing rope from his utility belt, Ezra had to holster his gun. He pressed his knee into the man's back, stowed his weapon, and tugged the rope out.

In a flash, the man moved, bringing his other arm beneath his body and rolling sideways to throw Ezra off balance, aided by the cumbersome weight of the backpack he still wore. He fell heavily to the ground, catching himself with an outstretched arm. His opponent lunged past, grabbing for the AK-47 still lying across the small clearing.

Ezra reacted instantly, shoving off the ground and propelling his weight forward to tackle the man before he could bring the assault rifle around to fire. They rolled, fighting for control of the gun, but the other man was taller and bigger, and the bulky backpack hindered Ezra's movements. In a moment the man had him pinned, his knee digging into Ezra's stomach.

He swallowed as the man brought the rifle around, the muzzle in his face. His first thought was of Sarah—he'd see her again soon. And his daughter. Their picture in his shirt pocket crinkled against his chest under the backpack strap.

But the next thought caught him off guard—what would happen to Haley when he was gone? Who would protect her?

Then Haley's voice rang out. "Get off him."

No.

She'd given up her hiding place. She stood in full sight, the AK-47 she'd been carrying now aimed at the man pinning him down.

The distraction was just enough to make the man's attention waver. With a grunt, Ezra grabbed the gun, jerked it toward the ground to loosen the man's grip and brought the butt up hard into the man's face. He yowled, rolling sideways as blood poured from his nose. A second blow was enough to knock him out completely.

Unbuckling the backpack straps across his chest, Ezra shook himself free and climbed to his feet. Haley hadn't moved, but even from here he could see the gun muzzle trembling in her hands.

"Did you take the safety off?" he asked, torn between anger and relief.

She shook her head, tilting the gun to the side to show the big metal lever still in place. The adrenaline diffusing from his system gave way to amusement and he laughed, shaking his head, as he dropped back down to his knees next to his pack.

"I can't believe that actually worked," he muttered. Then louder, "Don't ever try that again."

She collapsed next to him, setting the rifle on the ground. "You didn't exactly leave me any other option. I couldn't just sit by and let him kill you."

The way her voice was shaking made him want to pull her into a hug. Which was utterly ridiculous because he'd only hugged his sister and his nephews since Sarah. Instead, he settled for placing a hand on her shoulder, squeezing gently. "Well, I appreciate the concern. You're a brave woman. Although it would've been safer for you to stay hidden."

"Maybe. Or maybe he'd have found me next."

Her blue gaze was piercing, clear and strong like the sky on a bright summer day, and he suddenly found himself wondering if she was always this way, this intriguing mix of strength and vulnerability.

She blinked, and he realized that not only had he been staring, he still had his hand on her shoulder. He whipped it back and turned his attention to tying up the man using a length of rope.

"There, that should keep him in place for a while, long enough to give us a decent head start."

Haley bit her lip. "You don't have to help me. This is putting you in so much danger. I'm sure there are people who care about you, who wouldn't want to lose you…" Her voice trailed off as her gaze dropped to his empty left ring finger.

Nope. Not going there.

"Ha." He snorted. "As if I'd leave you to fend for yourself out here. Besides, whoever the newest Haley Whitcombe admirer is would never forgive me if something happened to you. He wouldn't be able to propose at a Mariners game."

Her cheeks turned pink, and for a moment he wondered if he'd pried too deep. "You heard about that?"

He nodded. "Yeah, sorry. It wasn't very sensitive of me to bring it up."

"Don't worry about it. It was a long time ago." Her shoulders drooped. "A classic example of my faulty judgment when it comes to men. I'm pretty sure Xander wouldn't have noticed if I went missing, so long as he was still in the spotlight."

"Then there's something seriously wrong with him," he said lightly, and she rewarded him with a smile.

Faulty judgment, huh? Was that why she hadn't had a relationship splattered across the news lately? Of course, Haley's love life was the last thing that should matter to him.

But maybe he'd misjudged her. Maybe she wasn't only a spoiled, demanding, big city heiress. If anything, she'd proven herself to be quite resilient so far. Courageous. And she had a sense of humor buried somewhere beneath all that stress and ambition.

He hoped however deep those traits ran, they'd be enough. Because they had a long way to go to get back to safety, and she was going to need every drop of resilience and courage she had.

FIVE

Ezra led the way deeper into the woods, keeping them on a course that would eventually intersect with the trail. The day had grown hotter as the sun climbed up above the trees and started its slow descent on the other side. Haley kept pace behind him, her leather jacket now tied around her waist. She'd pulled her hair back into a ponytail, though stray bits had escaped and clung to her cheeks, which were now red with exertion.

She hadn't complained once in the hours since their narrow escape. Merely followed his directions and let him take the lead. Impressive for someone so headstrong.

The going had gotten significantly slower in the last fifteen minutes, though, as the terrain on this side of the creek grew steeper. Time to drop down to the trail.

"Let's stop here for a moment," he said, taking off his pack. He offered Haley a protein bar then pulled out a topo map of the park. Holding it out, he pointed to Thunder Glacier. "Here's where your plane went down. We've been hiking here, parallel to this creek." He traced the route with his finger. "I'd guess the paratroopers dropped here, on the opposite ridge, and split up to search for us. They must know by now we got away, and if they have any idea about the park's layout and terrain, they'll know we're going to head north to the road."

She nodded, the frown deepening across her brow. "How can we avoid them?"

"We'll have to drop down to the trail for a while because it's getting too steep here, but once we pass this area—" he dragged a finger in a circle on the map "—we can ford the creek and do what we've been doing here, hiking off-trail but parallel." He scanned the sky, noting that the sun had slipped farther west. "I'm hoping we can make another four miles by dark. That'll give us about ten miles tomorrow until we reach the road."

"And then? How far to someplace with cell service?"

"My car is parked at the trailhead. I can take you back to the seasonal ranger housing in Newhalem. It's where I live out here when I'm not on backcountry patrol. There's a landline if your cell won't work. Or if you think it's being traced."

"Okay." Her throat bobbed and she looked down, suddenly absorbed in retying her jacket around her waist.

That strange compulsion to comfort her washed over Ezra again, but he gritted his teeth and kept his own hands busy folding the map and putting it back into the backpack. "You ready to keep going?"

"Of course." By the time she looked up, her face had cleared. No sign of weakness. Working in the corporate world, she was probably used to covering up her feelings. That and the fact she was always in the news. Before their daughter was born and Sarah decided to stay home, she'd worked as an elementary school teacher, and she'd always joke when she got home about taking off her "work mask." Haley's seemed permanently affixed to her face. It had to get itchy.

He repacked their nearly empty water bottles—they'd have to refill them in the creek using the built-in LifeStraws—and hoisted the pack into place. They picked their way in silence at an angle down the steep ridge toward the trail, slipping occasionally on loose patches of dirt, until they reached the bottom.

Here the trees gave way to a narrow dirt path running alongside Thunder Creek, which was just visible through a thin wall of trees separating it from the trail.

Ezra stopped again near the edge of the trail, looking both directions. The roar of the creek drowned out other sounds, but he didn't see anything unusual.

"Looks clear." He glanced at Haley, who'd stopped beside him. "If they find us, you *run*. Get yourself to cover. Don't worry about me. I'll keep them from chasing you as long as I can. Understood?"

Her lips parted, but before she said anything, he tugged the park map out again and pressed it into her hands. "Keep this just in case we get separated. If you can find the creek, you'll be able to get back to the road."

Nodding, she stuffed the map into the back pocket of her jeans, the camera shifting against her side. She could almost have passed as a tourist if not for the large gun on her back.

Ezra pointed to it now. "I'd better show you how that works. Just in case."

"Is that really necessary?" Haley's fingers played with the two straps where they crisscrossed over her sternum.

"If you end up on your own for any reason, yes."

She pulled the gun off, holding it out to him. He showed her how to maneuver the safety lever off and back on again, then made her do it herself until she could manage it without either flinching or straining.

"It's semiautomatic, so shooting is easy enough." He held up the gun to demonstrate how to handle it. "But don't take any shots unless absolutely necessary. You don't have any more magazines, and gunfire would be a dead giveaway of your location."

"I'm praying I never even have to take the safety off again." Haley offered him a weak smile. It wasn't much, just a tiny tilting up of her lips, but it brought light to her whole face. "But thank you. I feel a little safer."

He smiled back. "Good. I'm praying that too." Something sparked between them, a moment of solidarity and understanding that somehow felt both exciting and unsettling at the same time. It reminded him of the way he'd felt around Sarah when they first met, which probably explained why warning bells were going off in the back of his mind.

Sarah had been the love of his life—he wasn't supposed to feel that way ever again about someone else. Besides, now he knew the harsh truth. As much as he loved and trusted God, there was no guarantee He wouldn't strip away someone Ezra cared about like that again. Of course, it wasn't God's fault—they lived in a sinful world where bad things happened. But God could've stopped that driver from ramming into his wife's car and stealing her and their daughter's lives, and He hadn't.

All of which meant Ezra had to safeguard his own heart if he wanted to avoid that kind of pain again. He had a job to do now—get Haley back to civilization, and then she'd be out of his hands and his life.

He cleared his throat, adjusted his backpack and headed onto the trail. The sooner they got back to the road, the better.

Haley glanced behind them as she followed Ezra onto the trail, grateful to see no sign of movement. The big gun still dug into her back, but it felt less foreign now, like she didn't have to be afraid of it. And it had already saved their lives once.

The path was wide enough for two, but she let Ezra walk a half step ahead. He'd been a surprisingly patient teacher as her fingers fumbled to get the safety lever in and out of position. The interaction lent more evidence to her suspicion that outside of their dire situation, he was normally an easygoing, warmhearted person. She hadn't been around enough people like that for most of her life.

Her father was incredibly intelligent and driven—how else could he have made Whitcombe Aerotech into one of the country's foremost companies?—and for the most part he surrounded himself with similar people. Bright, accomplished, achievement-oriented. And Haley had fit right in. It'd been easy to see from early childhood what kinds of things brought her father's praise, and after her mother's death from cancer when she was in middle school, she'd been doubly motivated never to let her father down. His glowing praise had made her feel on top of the world, but his disappointment burned like an open wound that wouldn't heal. She'd had her first taste of it with Xander. Her father tolerated but never really liked the businessman. Xander wasn't good enough for his daughter. In the end, he'd been right.

Well, she was in for a heap of disappointment now. But what galled her most was that her father would probably give Chris the job instead, trusting the company he'd built from scratch to an unethical criminal. Part of her wondered if Chris had stolen from Whitcombe Aerotech before—after all, if he was willing to do it now, why not earlier? Like that incident four years ago when a competitor scooped the fuel injector she'd been working on.

That was the last project in which she'd done real research, before her father moved her over to the business management side of things. Her heart twinged with an unexpected sense of loss as memories played through her mind—the thrill of discovery, the delight of being fully absorbed by some problem, the camaraderie of the research team. Sometimes she forgot how much she'd lost by moving out of R&D and into the corporate office.

Or how much loneliness gnawed at her heart with no one to open up to. Be real around. She'd shared more with Ezra these past few hours than she had with anyone in a long time.

A tree root snagged the toe of her boot and she nearly missed a step. *Better pay more attention.* Maybe being stuck out here, with Chris trying to steal her job, was God's way of reminding her to be grateful for what she had and not complain.

"You okay?" Ezra's low, soothing voice cut across her thoughts.

"Yeah, just stumbled."

He frowned as he scanned her face, and she had the

sudden urge to hide behind the nearest rock. Instead, she covertly wiped at her cheeks, checking her fingers for stray mascara. None of it seemed to be coming off, but how long ago had she applied it?

"How long have you been awake?" he demanded.

"Since—" she did a quick tally in her head "—5:00 a.m. yesterday? I think that's right."

He pressed his lips together. "No wonder you look so exhausted."

Irritation gurgled in Haley's stomach. He didn't have any right to judge. "I have a stressful job. I don't sleep very well. And if I hadn't gone into the office in the middle of the night, I never would've figured out what Chris was up to. Not all of us get to relax out here in the woods every day." She waved an arm at their surroundings.

Somehow she'd either picked up her pace or he had slowed down, because now they were keeping stride with each other. He threw her a sideways glance, one eyebrow raised. "Relax? Really? This is like a vacation for you or something?"

Was he offended? If so, he deserved it. But no, that was definitely humor dancing in those brown eyes, and the corners of his mouth tilted up in a secret smile. For one brief moment she wished she could hear him laugh, but then she shook it off. Ridiculous.

"No, this is *not* like a vacation." Though frankly she wasn't quite sure what a real vacation would be like. Her parents had taken her to the beach once, but that had been so long ago she could scarcely remember it. "I'm sorry, I shouldn't have said it. I'm just…tired." *Way to state the obvious, Haley.* She averted her gaze to her feet, watching the scuffed, brown toes of her boots as she stepped over a rock half-buried in the path.

"Hey, it's cool. So, if this job is so stressful, why do you do it? Because of your dad?"

"I guess." She looked up, taking in the graceful arch of the tree branches over the path and the way the dappled light glittered on the nearby stream. It *was* beautiful out here, something she'd hardly had a chance to appreciate so far. And quiet. No phone notifications or bus engines or hum of electricity. Just the wind in the branches, gurgling water and the sound of their feet on the packed earth. "I kind of grew up under the expectation I'd work with him one day, especially when they saw I had a head for math and science. After Mom passed, it just seemed like there wasn't another option, not really."

She glanced at Ezra and shrugged. A shadow flitted across his features, like she'd tapped into some unspoken pain, but it was gone again so fast she wondered if she'd imagined it.

"I'm sorry about your mom." His voice was raspy, and he cleared his throat. "How old were you?"

"Sixth grade, so...ten?"

His eyebrows pinched together. "Isn't that a little young for middle school?"

"I skipped third and fourth grades. I was getting bored in class and causing trouble for the teacher, so they moved me up to..." Haley's voice trailed off and she clapped her mouth shut. What had gotten into her? She *never* told men about her accomplishments, especially good-looking, single ones. They either turned tail and ran or faked interest long enough to get the fame they wanted. Like Xander.

But the look on Ezra's face—a curious mix of amusement and respect—didn't fit either profile, rather like the man himself. He was unlike anyone she'd ever met. Not interested in her fame or what she could do for him, but content with his own life. And handsome, in a rugged way that made him look like he'd stepped out of a North Face ad.

"Wait a sec, *you* were causing trouble?" His eyes sparkled, as if this were the most entertainment he'd had in weeks. "Miss High Profile, I've Got It All Together Haley Whitcombe? What were you doing, staring out the window? Passing notes to your friends?"

If only... Passing notes would've been a lot more normal. She pressed her lips together, hoping maybe he'd drop it. Nope. He was still watching her expectantly.

Fine. "At first I was working ahead in the textbooks, but the teacher wanted me to pay attention, so she made me keep my books in my desk."

"And...?"

She let out a huff. This was going to sound hopelessly nerdy. "I started making up my own equations to solve. On the top of the desk. In pencil."

"Equations? As in algebra?"

"Yeah." She winced. "I checked out an algebra textbook from the library."

He didn't laugh, and for a moment Haley couldn't tell if she was disappointed or relieved. But the admiration that flashed on his face was almost more unsettling. Because it looked genuine. "Haley, that is seriously impressive. My oldest nephew is a third grader, and we can't get him to check out anything harder than an easy reader."

The heat in her neck flared up to her cheeks. Time

to divert this conversation away from *her*. "Sounds like he's right on track, then. How many nephews do you have?"

"Two. They're seven and five years old. A real handful for my sister." His mouth tilted in a crooked smile and he looked down at the path, as if lost in some pleasant memory.

"Do you see them often?"

"Eh, not really. My sister and her husband live down in Portland. She's always inviting me to come, especially since—" He coughed, cutting himself off. "It's hard for me to get away from work."

"But isn't your job here seasonal?"

He nodded. "Yeah. The park basically shuts down in winter because of snow. I work for Seattle PD the rest of the year."

Seattle. How far away did he live from Haley? Did his cruiser ever drive past her high-rise apartment? Or Whitcombe Aerotech? Funny how the world could seem so big and yet so small at the same time.

She shook the thought away. Where Ezra Dalton lived was totally irrelevant to her life. It wasn't like they were going to keep in touch after this wild escapade ended. After all, no matter how genuine and kind Ezra seemed, she'd deluded herself into believing the best about Xander too. Her decision-making in the romance department was questionable, at best.

"I probably owe them a visit," he muttered, almost as if speaking to himself. He wrapped his left hand around the backpack strap where it crossed his uniform pocket. After a moment, he pulled the hand away and turned back to Haley. "What about you? Any little nieces or nephews?"

She shook her head. "I'm an only child. My father has an older sister—my aunt Lissy—but she's it for extended family." Probably a good thing, because she'd never keep up with family obligations on top of her job. Although after seeing that secret smile on Ezra's face, she couldn't help wondering what she might be missing out on.

Ezra grew silent as the trail reached the end of the steep ridge they'd been following and turned downward in series of sharp switchbacks. He took the lead, his expression serious as he scanned their surroundings. The creek churned to the right, louder now, with foaming white rapids cascading past boulders as it descended the rocky slope.

Haley hugged her arms across her stomach, chilled despite the heat. Though it wasn't that hot now, she realized. In the hours since they'd escaped the glacier, the sun had peaked and was now sliding toward the other horizon, leaving long shadows across the path. A little breeze danced over her cheeks, lifting stray strands of her hair and carrying a hint of icy mountain peaks. She paused, slipping her jacket back on.

Night was coming. They'd be sleeping out here, surrounded by pitch darkness and wild animals and armed men with guns.

How much longer before they were caught?

SIX

Ezra hated the low visibility on these switchbacks, and the way Thunder Creek had them hemmed in almost completely on one side. They had, by his estimation, half a mile left before the trail would level out near the old Skagit mine. Then there'd be a long, steady descent followed by a climb up to where they'd camp. The nine miles back to his car from there would be mainly flat, easygoing woodland trail.

If they could just stay ahead of their pursuers.

So far God had granted them mercy, allowing them to escape twice. But the third time? He wasn't so sure. Even though he'd been up before dawn, he was used to this kind of terrain and long hours of hiking. But not Haley, not after what she'd been through. How much longer could they keep up this pace?

She'd been, quite frankly, amazing. Never complaining, even though she had to be footsore and hungry and exhausted. She'd matched strides with him all afternoon, but one look at her was enough for even a rookie ranger to see she needed sleep. And from the way his own stomach was growling, they both needed a meal. The body could only keep going for so long on reserves.

As they rounded the next hairpin turn, he froze, listening. Some stray sound had caught his ear, something other than creek and wind in the trees. Haley stopped next to him, her face drawn as she clutched the straps crisscrossed over her collarbone. He held up his hand before she could speak.

There it was again, coming from above. He leaned against the embankment, gesturing for Haley to do the same. Then, stepping up on a large rock, he craned his neck to see the path. At first, there was nothing, and he nearly hopped down to keep going. But then his eyes picked up what his instincts had already observed. Movement through the trees—barely visible because of the dark green clothes, until a flash of skin appeared briefly.

The paratroopers.

He gritted his teeth and perched on the rock a moment longer, trying to get a count, but it was impossible through the trees. Definitely more than one. When he dropped back down next to Haley, she raised a questioning eye.

"It's them," he whispered. "Maybe four switchbacks up the hill. They haven't seen us yet or they'd be shooting."

Her throat bobbed. "What do we do?"

He glanced down the path. "Keep going. Stick close to the inside edge of the trail. Once the path leaves the trees… We'll think of something."

They pushed on, down the next length, around a hairpin bend, then down again. Over and over. Each misstep sent a shower of gravel rolling down the path that felt as loud as an avalanche. Ezra kept glancing up the hillside, checking the progress of the camo-clad figures.

He couldn't be positive, but it looked like their pursuers were gaining. Probably because they didn't have to hug the inner edge of the path or duck and run to avoid notice at the turns.

A sinking feeling filled his stomach when they rounded the next turn. This switchback was longer than the others by at least double, and partway down the trees gave way to an expanse of open hillside dotted with wildflowers. At the far end, a spur of the trail led to the next horse camp, but the main path kept zigzagging down the face of the exposed ridge. A few large rocks might provide a bit of cover, but nothing like what they'd need.

Haley stopped, glancing back at him with a pinched face. "Now what?"

His mind whirred through the options. Keep going and hope for the best? Cut across the switchbacks and try to outrun them? Take up position behind a rock and try to get the jump on them? Nothing sounded safe.

But…what if they could hide long enough to let the men pass?

To their right, a rocky incline led upward to a ridge of trees. The creek churned somewhere close on the other side. If they could get out of sight, there was a chance the men would walk right on by, never knowing their quarry was so close.

The plan wasn't perfect, but it was a whole lot better than racing downhill with armed men at your back, especially when said pursuers had the high ground.

"This way." He pointed toward the incline. When the men above were out of sight, he scrambled up the small ridge, Haley following close behind.

Over the top, the incline wasn't as steep as it had

been on the trail side and the creek was a whole lot closer than Ezra had anticipated. Maybe a dozen feet? Trees and scattered rocks dotted the space between the crest of the ridge and the churning glacial water. He dropped to his knees, dipping his head low to the ground.

"It's no good," Haley said, her voice tight. She crouched next to him, her gaze darting from the switchbacks above to the trail leading away from where they knelt. "Even if we laid flat. The incline isn't enough."

"No, it's not." He clenched one hand as he rose from the ground. A random passerby might not notice, but anyone paying attention would. "Time for plan B."

She raised a questioning eyebrow, but he merely gestured for her to follow as he crossed the distance to the water's edge. The creek had gained in volume as it descended from its origins up in the glacial valley, and with the gradient of the ridge here, it rushed past in a milky blue torrent that sent splatters onto his face and shirt.

Her nose crinkled the way it did anytime she was about to argue. "You don't expect us to jump in there, do you?"

"Of course not. Not unless we absolutely have to." He scanned the bank, looking for any place two people might conceal themselves for a few minutes without falling in. Up and down in both directions, boulders jutted into the creek between patches of mud, and in a few places the bank rose above the water far enough someone might conceivably be able to hide.

"Ezra, look!" Haley urged, and he followed her outstretched finger to see the dark green shapes moving on the next switchback above them. One more turn, and they'd be headed straight for him and Haley.

A vise gripped his ribs. "We're out of time. You go there." He pointed a few feet upstream to a flat rock embedded in the creek's edge near a place where the bank rose. Haley should just be able to fit if she huddled down, and with the incline from the trail, she'd be impossible to see. "If for some reason you do end up in the water, remember to keep your feet downstream and head for the opposite shore."

"What about you?"

"Just go. I'll come up with something."

She crawled onto the rock while he picked his way downstream, keeping low to the ground. A boulder stood on the edge fifteen feet from Haley's rock, and at its base, water splashed over a couple of smaller rocks. Not exactly the ideal spot to stand, but he didn't have much choice.

The first of the men rounded the far turn of the switchback, his face a floating speck beneath dark hair. The man was watching the trail, but any second now, he could look up and see Ezra's face. Maybe even a flash of green backpack.

Ezra offered a quick prayer for safety, then gripped the rough boulder and stepped out onto the slick rock. Not optimal, but it would work. He hoped.

He nearly slipped as the heavy backpack threw him off balance, but he dug his fingertips into the boulder until they ached. Haley's eyes went wide. He offered a quick shrug, then felt for a decent grip on another rock with his other foot. He tried to crouch, but the slightest movement threatened to throw him off balance again, so he settled for pressing his face and chest as close as he could to the boulder. Water splashed and churned around his boots, soaking his pants.

As his gaze dragged along the edge of the bank, tension wrapped around his chest. He'd jumped down here from a patch of gravel on the bank. But farther upstream, Haley's footprints were clearly visible in the mud. What if they'd left more tracks near the trail?

He swallowed, tightening his grip on the boulder, and prayed nobody noticed.

Haley crouched on the flat rock at the edge of the rushing water, her heart pounding. She prayed the men wouldn't see them, that they'd walk past without checking up here, but her prayers felt like they were bouncing off a glass ceiling. After all, why had God allowed her to end up in this mess anyway?

She'd poured everything out trying to make everyone happy, including God. Church every Sunday—she even volunteered in the nursery—a Bible study at work with some sweet women from marketing, and *all* those charity functions. The equation wasn't complicated—she served and followed God, and He blessed her. Wasn't that the deal?

Well, she wasn't feeling very blessed at the moment. Icy water splashed her face and clothes as she crouched, the jacket tightly wrapped over the camera to protect it. Sure, their pursuers hadn't found them yet, but what good would that do when she died of hypothermia? Or fell in the creek and hit her head on a rock? Or withered away from starvation?

She glanced at Ezra, perched on rocks in the stream, arms wrapped around a boulder. His face was hidden beneath the brim of his hat, but she imagined he looked as calm and collected as always. Unflappable—that was the word she wanted—like nothing ever bothered him. She imagined his faith in God must be exactly the same. *He* never felt like he had to earn God's grace, or that God was punishing him. No, all this torture he was facing had been brought on by Haley.

Her knees ached from the awkward position, and her hands were going numb from bracing her body against the cold rock. How much longer would they have to crouch like this? And then what? Would they ever escape these men and get back to civilization? Or was God going to hand out the ultimate punishment and let her die out here?

What did she do wrong, anyway?

Before she could consider the possible answers, a shout from nearby locked her already frozen joints in place. The sound was barely audible over the rushing of the creek. She glanced again at Ezra, who peeked at the path. The way his expression shifted said it all—the men had figured out where they'd left the trail.

He didn't look at her, but his fingers on his left hand waved ever so slightly as if to say, "keep down." A warning she hardly needed.

A long, tense moment passed until she could *feel* them up on the bank, like cold shadows hovering above her, sending a chill coursing down her spine. Then they were gone, moving downstream, and she let out a small sigh.

The relief didn't last.

"You, come up on the bank. Now!" The voice wasn't talking to her—it came from too far downstream. From her vantage point pressed against the cold bank, Haley could only make out a pair of camo-clad arms aiming a gun at Ezra. Cold sweat broke out on her back. After everything he'd gone through for her...

Please, God, no. I'm sorry I complained, sorry I brought this on him. Ezra didn't do anything wrong.

His knuckles whitened where he clutched the rock and he slowly raised his head, never once casting a glance in her direction. At least they hadn't shot him on sight—that meant they wanted him alive. For now.

To help find Haley? Her throat squeezed.

And he would go with them. He'd give himself up in the hope they wouldn't find her hiding place. She'd be left alone out here in the wilderness. The tightness knotting up her insides was unbearable. When he refused to help them find her...

They'd kill him.

Unless she did something. *Now.* What good was keeping herself alive and out of jail at the expense of someone else's life?

"Wait!" Her voice cut through the churning of the creek and the soft sounds of nature. Staying hunched on her knees, she leaned out to see the men on the bank.

Three of them. Their guns were on Ezra, but now, quick as lightning, they turned to her. She lifted her hands in the air, glancing at Ezra's still form against the boulder. His brown eyes burned with intensity as he met her gaze, and from the way his jaw muscle flexed, he was angry.

Tough. She wasn't going to let him die for her.

He shook his head, ever so slightly, then glanced down at his feet. Like he was trying to tell her something. What?

"Stand up," one of the men ordered her. "Nice and slow. Hands where we can see them."

Obediently she raised her hands. Downstream, Ezra shifted his back foot, letting it slide closer to the edge of the rock until the toe of his boot was pointing at the churning water. The men, all their attention on Haley, paid him no heed as he stared at her, his eyes practically boring a hole through her head.

When he shook his foot again, realization dawned with a cold sense of terror.

He was going to jump into the water, and he wanted her to follow.

"Get moving!" one of the men barked.

Haley swallowed. Made eye contact with Ezra. "Okay, I'll do it."

He flashed a thumbs-up with his free hand. Then, with a loud cry sure to draw the men's attention, he flailed his arms away from the boulder in the perfect imitation of an accidental fall. But he kept that right foot firmly planted in place until the last second, when he propelled himself away from the rocks and jumped feetfirst into the rushing water.

She didn't allow herself the luxury of hesitation. Before he'd even completed the jump, before the men had a chance to react, Haley slid sideways off her rock and into the icy torrent.

SEVEN

The water was so cold, it stole the breath from Haley's lungs. On the bank, the men moved in a blur of motion then vanished as the current rushed her downstream past Ezra's boulder. Immediately she fumbled beneath her jacket for the camera, struggling to hold it above the water. What mattered now was keeping the SD card intact.

That meant not slamming into one of the rocks jutting in the middle of the creek, so she swiveled her feet around to the front. Just in time—her boots pummeled into a rock barely submerged beneath the surface, sending a jolt of pain up her shins, and she pushed off to the side. The current sucked her past so quickly it was disorienting. With effort she righted herself, getting her feet aimed back downstream, preparing to dodge the next rock.

Up ahead, a bright green pack bobbed in the water, Ezra's cap visible just above it. He worked his way to the right, stopping against a rock embedded in the opposite bank. Sitting in the creek with his back against the rock, he waved and called her name.

Another rock was coming up fast, right in front of

her, and if Haley didn't time her push correctly, she'd end up going left and missing Ezra. Tension knotted up her insides as she braced for impact. Her feet connected with the rock and she fought the current, successfully swinging her body to the right. But she was still so far away from the bank, and—

Why did the water vanish up ahead, where it narrowed between those two rocks?

The roar filling her ears said enough. *Waterfall.* She gulped, nearly submerging the camera by accident as she struggled to pull herself closer to the bank. There was motion again on the opposite side, a blur of dark green moving against the trees and rocks. A second later something pelted the side of her face. Not a bullet—she was still here, still battling the current to get to Ezra's outstretched hand. Must've been splintered chips of rock, cut loose by gunfire she couldn't hear over the noise of the water.

Then Ezra's hand snagged her arm where she held the camera above the churning torrent. He heaved her in closer to the bank as she kicked against the slippery rocks on the creek bed.

"Come on," he grunted, the tendons in his neck standing out.

"I'm trying." She slipped, nearly losing her footing, but flung her free hand toward Ezra and latched her fingers around the strap of his pack.

As soon as she was close enough, he wrapped both hands around her arms and tossed her to the bank. Just in time too, because bullets sprayed across the creek where she'd been seconds before, sending up a shower of water.

"Hurry!" she called, turning back to tug at his arm.

He clambered up beside her as the next stream of bullets ricocheted off the rock. Rock chips exploded around them, and Haley smothered a scream. They lurched forward, dropping to hands and knees, and scurried up the bank to the relative safety of the tree line.

"There!" He pointed to a boulder a little farther downstream. Bullets bit into the bank behind them, tracking across the area where they'd been moving only seconds before.

Tense as a taut spring—that was how she felt. She clutched her hands to the back of her head, even though it was ridiculous to think that would save her from the rain of death nipping at their heels. Then Ezra was shoving her down to crouch in the temporary shelter of the big rock and wedging himself next to her so close their arms and shoulders touched. The contact sent a little flush of welcome warmth through her freezing body. Sure, she barely knew him, but they'd saved each other's lives again—for the moment, anyway. Their eyes met and a spark passed between them, making her suddenly light-headed. Concern, solidarity, but maybe something more, far stronger than anything she'd felt with Xander. Something she didn't know what to do with.

Then gunfire raked the opposite side of the rock and the moment broke as she tucked herself into a tighter ball. "Are they crossing the creek?"

Ezra leaned away from her, glancing around the side of the rock. Answering gunfire made him whip back around. Bullets pummeled into the other side of the rock. "No, not yet."

Frayed green fabric stuck up at odd angles on the top of his backpack. She brushed stiff fingers across the damage. Bullet holes. He'd come within inches of being shot in the head. Her mouth went dry. "They hit your pack. Are you okay?"

He craned his neck around, trying to see the damage. "Yeah, for the moment."

"Why were they shooting at us?" she asked, half to herself.

Ezra frowned. "They're trying to kill us?"

"No. I mean, yes, but the first guy who caught me said they were supposed to make it look like an accident. I think that's why they didn't shoot us right away back there, because they had some other plan to dispose of us."

"Maybe because we escaped? They're supposed to make it look like an accident if possible, but definitely not let us get away? Regardless, we'd better get moving. It won't be long before they find somewhere to cross. Keep that rock behind you and stay down low."

A reminder she didn't need, not with those holes in his pack only inches from the back of his head. The could've-beens knotted up inside her stomach…her left out here alone, and Ezra… He would've given his life saving a woman wanted for murder and espionage, a woman he didn't even know. When was the last time she'd met anyone so selfless?

"Haley?" His voice cut into her thoughts and she blinked. Concern flickered in his dark gaze. "You ready?"

She nodded, a tremor running through her shoulders as if she could physically shake off the horrible thoughts. It didn't work. Instead, a chill settled deep in her bones.

"You go first." His gentle tone made her feel even

worse. She'd done nothing to deserve his help or kindness—nothing but put his life in danger.

She kept her face down and away from his penetrating gaze as she crawled up the slope. Sharp pine needles and hard bits of rock dug into her hands and knees. Behind them, another round of gunfire broke out, making her flinch, but she forced herself to keep crawling until she crested the next ridge.

When she paused to glance back, Ezra stopped too. The boulder they'd hidden behind, and beyond it the churning creek, were no longer visible. He climbed hesitantly to his feet, then motioned for her to stand too.

"We're clear for now." He pointed ahead, into the forest where the incline dropped steeply to the left. "We need to head north, parallel to the creek and the trail down below."

Her knees trembled, but this time it wasn't fear, it was exhaustion. And cold. She wasn't sure she'd ever felt so cold in her life, not even that time she went to a winter charity ball in a sleeveless gown. It didn't help that they were fully in the shade beneath the trees, and the day was growing late. In places where the sun could break through the canopy, the light seemed feeble and red-tinged, like it had used its last strength trying to get to her.

Was she using up her last strength too?

"Hey." Ezra's gentle rumble pulled her back out of herself. His face was lined with concern, and she made an effort to stand straighter. Pull herself together. People relied on Haley Whitcombe—she was the CEO's daughter, the one who had the answers—she didn't have room for weakness. Her father's words came back to her. *Even if you don't know or you're having a rotten*

day or you feel like crying, save it till you get home.
People are counting on you, Haley, and you have a re-
sponsibility to be strong.

He'd said that the morning after she broke up with
Xander in front of a hot dog stand at that baseball game.
The photos were plastered all over the tabloids. At the
time, she'd been crushed—but in hindsight, she could
see how the heartbreak was more over the death of the
dream of finding "the one" than because of her feelings for Xander. One glance from Ezra, and the way
her whole being lit up told her she'd seriously under-
estimated the giddy delight of falling for somebody.

Wait a sec. *No way.* She had *not* meant that. At all.
Nobody was falling for anybody out here. The stress of
the situation was messing with her brain.

"I'm fine. Let's get going." Her lower lip was trembling, so she bit it. Folded her arms tighter across her
chest.

He reached a hand toward her—*almost* as if he were
going to pull her into an embrace—but then the hand
dropped back to his side. A foreign emotion flitted
through her chest at the sight of those fingers curling
next to his leg, almost like some foolish part of her had
wanted him to wrap his arms around her. The part of
her that had forgotten how she'd sworn off romance.

"We'll rest soon," he said, "after we get some distance from them."

She followed him through the trees, ducking beneath
branches, stumbling over roots. The straps of the camera and gun dug into her shoulders, chafing her skin
where the jacket was open over her collarbone. She
hadn't tried turning the camera on yet, but at least it
didn't appear to be dripping. Unlike the rest of her.

A cool breeze danced through the trees. It would've felt fresh and pleasant after a normal day of hiking, but now, with her clothes soaked through and her body reaching its limits, goose bumps prickled across her skin. What she wouldn't give for a hot shower, a meal and her bed with its down comforter.

A sob built in her chest and she gritted her teeth, determined not to let it escape. The last time she'd cried in front of anyone else she'd been twelve, standing beside her mother's casket at the funeral. Her dad had held her tightly, letting her cry it all out. Then he'd wiped away the tears with his thumb, his own face stoic, and said, "That's all now, Haley girl. Your mom is counting on you. So am I."

She'd simply have to ignore these foreign feelings of weakness, this strange urge to step into that man's arms and let him shield her from the terrors of the world. She'd gotten along just fine before, and she would now too. As soon as they could get back to the road and she called Ford, she and this camera would be headed back to Seattle to unravel Chris's plans, and this nightmare in the Cascades would be over and forgotten.

But as she trudged next to Ezra, she wasn't entirely convinced she'd be able to forget *him*.

Ezra hooked his fingers through the straps of his pack and kept his focus on the ground. Haley walked a pace behind, letting him choose the best path through the tangle of undergrowth and gnarled roots jutting out of the pine needle–covered ground. They'd been heading due north for nearly an hour now with no sign of their pursuers. He guessed the men had chosen to descend the ridge and look for an easier place to cross the creek, but it'd only be a matter of time before they were back on the same side.

He and Haley had the harder going. Down below at the base of the ridge, the trail ran alongside the creek on a flat stretch of marsh for a few miles before climbing back up. But up here where they were, the ridge rose sharply to a spur running north of Mount Logan. Cutting sideways across it meant walking at an awkward angle and continually fighting gravity's pull down the slope.

And Haley had him worried. Her breath came in sharp little puffs from behind him, and more than once when he'd glanced back, he'd caught her massaging a stitch in her side. She'd drop her hand and straighten her face as soon as she noticed he was looking, like it wasn't okay to admit she was exhausted.

He still wasn't sure what had happened near the creek, when he'd come *this* close to pulling her into an embrace. Like some instinct to comfort had taken over. Thankfully reason had intervened and stopped him before he actually did it. Based on that video footage she'd shown him, he was convinced she was innocent. But still...

That was no reason to *hold* her. The mere fact he'd wanted to made him feel guilty, like he was betraying Sarah's memory. He shook away the thought, focusing instead on what needed to be done to keep them alive.

Like getting some rest. And food. Hunger ripped through his gut like a savage beast trying to shred his insides, letting out a low gurgling growl.

"What was that?" Haley's eyes were wide as her gaze darted back and forth.

Uh, his stomach? Did she really think it was a wild

animal? Fighting to keep the smile off his face, he paused and looked around. "What? Did you hear something?"

"What kinds of animals live out here?" Her voice wavered ever so slightly.

She'd probably kill him later, but he couldn't stop himself. "Oh, tons of big predators. This is one of the few sanctuaries left for them in the lower forty-eight since it's so remote. Brown and black bears, gray wolves, cougars, bobcats, wolverines… I'm surprised we haven't run into any yet."

His stomach gurgled again, and the fear in her expression shifted into a scowl. "That's *not* funny."

"I thought it was." He couldn't stop his lips from quirking, even more so when her nose crinkled. Probably hardly been teased in her life. "Those animals *are* out here. They just usually steer clear of people. I take it you don't get out of the city much?"

"Not hiking." She glanced up at the leafy canopy far above their heads. "I prefer to fly."

He winced, thinking of the wreckage on the glacier. "Was that *your* plane?"

"Yep. A Cessna 172 Skyhawk. My first major purchase after I started working full-time for my dad."

"Like before a house or a car?"

She nodded. "I've got a place in downtown Seattle now, in one of the new towers, but I rented for a long time. And—" her voice dropped off and she blushed "—I just bought the car recently. I can call a company car and driver anytime I want, so it felt kind of like a luxury having my own."

Wow. To be so well off. He thought back to his and Sarah's little fixer-upper on Seattle's west side, their one car under the carport, the worn sofa they'd been saving up to replace. The house now belonged to another starry-eyed young couple and the car was rusting in a junkyard somewhere, totaled in the wreck that had robbed him and Sarah of the future they'd planned. His stomach growled again, but this time he didn't feel like laughing.

"Can I ask you something?" Haley said.

No. He shrugged. "Aren't you tired?"

"Talking keeps me going. What made you want to come out here? I mean, it's beautiful, but it's so remote. Do you miss the city? Or being near your family?" Her lips parted, like she wanted to ask more, but she stayed silent.

It had been a long time since anybody asked him about his personal life. Back at the precinct everybody knew about the accident, and out here, life revolved around the park and the job, not the lives the rangers left behind. How long could he put off telling her about what had happened?

"Sure, I miss my sister and her kids. But the city is…stressful. Full of memories." Wrong thing to say. Her eyebrows lifted, but she let him keep talking. "Out here, I feel like it's just me and God and the world He created."

"I can see that." She said it slowly, hesitatingly, like she knew there was more to the story and she was trying to figure out how to pry it from him. Now would be the right moment to deflect and change the subject, but some traitorous part of him almost hoped she'd ask. Like everything bottled up inside was fighting to get out. Not that he would ever give in, in a million years.

But before he could think of a way to redirect, she

went on. "Bad memories? I suppose they must be, or you wouldn't be hiding out here in the middle of nowhere."

Hiding? Hold up, this woman had just met him. Where did she get the right to judge? "I'm not hiding. I *like* it out here. Besides, *you're* the one on the run from the law."

Her posture went rigid as they slipped and scrambled along the rocky ridge. "That's only temporary. Before long, I'll get this evidence to my dad's lawyer and this whole mess will be ironed out. I'll be back in Seattle where I belong, and you can get back to your happy, lonely life of stargazing and picking up litter, or whatever it is you normally do out here."

Ouch. Knife to the chest. Where did she get off mocking his occupation? The irritation that had been growing over the last few minutes threatened to burst out. Normally he'd do just about anything to avoid conflict, but for some reason Haley could knock it out of him at the drop of a hat. "What I do out here is keep people alive, particularly the ones who show up overconfident and unprepared." He gave her a pointed look, and though she stared at her feet, red crept into her cheeks.

But when she finally met his gaze, her jaw was set. "It's not like I came out here by choice. I fully acknowledge I need your help. What do you want, for me to grovel?"

"Nooo." He dragged the word out. "I want you to stop pretending like you've got it all together and admit—" He cut himself off. Admit what, exactly? That she was just as big of a mess as he was? Because this wasn't really about the exterior, was it? It was about what was inside, the heart. His was a broken, grieving wreck, and he had every right to keep it hidden. But at least he wasn't acting like everything was fine.

Unless...maybe she *did* have it all together. But part of him knew that wasn't true; it couldn't be—not with the way she'd talked about doing what her father wanted. Her whole world seemed to revolve around his company, not what *she* wanted out of life. And that mess with the near-fiancé a few years ago, that had to hurt. Haley wasn't a robot.

"Admit what?" she demanded.

"Nothing." He sighed. "Forget I said anything." As awkward silence descended over them, he wanted to kick himself for stirring up this ants' nest. What did Haley's personal life have to do with him anyway? Within twenty-four hours he'd get her back to the trail-head and arrange for her to leave, and she'd walk out of his life forever.

Which was good. Exactly what he wanted.

He didn't want to tell her about Sarah and Kaitlyn anyway. Because for some reason, talking to her felt too much like an open invitation to whatever had sparked between them earlier, and that door was staying firmly shut.

EIGHT

No reason to worry about wild animals now, Haley thought. Not with the way Ezra was practically stomping through the woods. She felt bad about it—at least, a little. She hadn't meant to attack what he chose to do for a living. God made all kinds of people and they each fit different jobs. But it was clear as daylight that he wasn't out here only because he liked the wilderness.

No, the man had something big going on underneath that warm, capable exterior, some hurt he was nursing, and if he didn't get it out, it was going to fester and eat him up inside.

She let out a small sigh. *Drop it, Haley.* It wasn't her job to help him. What she'd said was true—they'd split ways before long, and she'd be headed back to Seattle with Ford. That uncomfortable feeling prickling her insides was caused by exhaustion and stress. It didn't have anything to do with this handsome, strong, hurting ranger. Or his angry words.

I want you to stop pretending you've got it all together.

But didn't everybody do that? On some level? She had an image to maintain—that fact had been drilled into her since childhood. And it wasn't like whining and complaining was going to help them right now.

He'd cut himself off, but what had he meant to say?

And why did he care? Why did it matter to him how she acted or what she did?

Maybe it didn't matter—that was why he hadn't finished the question. Maybe she was reading into things, and all he wanted was to unload her onto Ford or the police so he wouldn't be responsible for her anymore.

The prickling inside veered perilously close to disappointment, a feeling that was far more unsettling, so she turned her attention to the sprawling wilderness around them. Despite their growing distance from the creek, the air had kept its dampness, and the scent of water mingled with evergreens and soft earth. As the ridge dropped in elevation, she recognized more deciduous trees mixed in with the firs. Ezra could probably tell her the names of all of them, but she wasn't going to ask.

Instead, she listened to the birds and the rustling of the leaves in the breeze as the sun dropped closer to the horizon. Light trickled through the canopy like soft, golden drops. Before long, it would be night. A chill wrapped itself around her still-damp clothes, and she stuck her hands into her pockets. At least the men hadn't found them again yet.

Hours passed before Ezra finally stopped. They'd descended for a long time, but they'd been climbing again for the last hour, and her legs felt like dead weights as she stumbled along in a haze of starvation and exhaustion.

Now he surveyed the small clearing where they stood, nodded briefly and unbuckled his pack. "This will do. I need a rest, and you look like a walking corpse."

She opened her mouth to object but gave up at the light dancing in his eyes. He had a sense of humor—she'd give him that. Besides, he was probably right. Thankfully there wasn't a mirror around here. "I've been up for thirty-six hours, and I was in a plane crash this morning. Cut a zombie some slack."

His grin lit up his whole face as he dug into his pack and started pulling things out. A miniature metal cooking pot. Silverware clipped together on a ring. A tiny metal canister. Something that looked a whole lot like a…

"Is that a Bunsen burner?" she asked.

"Camp stove. For backpacking. But same concept." They crouched on the soft forest dirt, and he showed her how to hook up the fuel can and light it. After filling the cooking pot with water, he set it on the burner to heat and rummaged in the bag again. When he turned to her, he held up two blue, plastic pouches. "Since you're my guest, you get first pick."

She read the labels over the pictures. "Chili mac. Or…chili. Big selection."

"Can't be too choosy when you're out here. Besides, they all pretty much taste the same anyway."

"In that case, I'll take the chili." Her stomach growled at the thought, and she stole a sideways glance at Ezra to catch him laughing. When was the last time she'd been this hungry? Normally she was so busy she scarcely gave food a thought.

While the water heated, he pulled out a small tarp and laid it on the ground to give them something to sit on. "I've got a tent, but I'm hesitant to set it up. It'd make us more visible."

"Guess that means no fire, either." She sat, tucking her knees under her chin and wrapping her arms around her legs. The tarp didn't do much to make the ground either softer or warmer.

"Sorry. I wish we could risk it. I know it's cold." He sat down next to her, a respectful distance away, but Haley couldn't help wishing he'd slide closer. Just for the warmth, of course.

"Can I take the gun off now?" The thing had been digging into her back all day.

He nodded. "But keep it close."

It was a sobering reminder, and she shivered.

Ezra dug into the pack again—it seemed bottomless, with how many items it held—and pulled out a navy blue stuff sack. "Here. Take my sleeping bag. You can slide into it to stay warm. I was going to let you sleep in it anyway."

"Thanks," she murmured, accepting it from him. She tugged off her boots, disgusted at her wet, stinky socks, now bearing patches of blood on the heels where her skin had rubbed raw.

"Here." A pair of clean socks hovered in front of her face, followed by Band-Aids. "They might be too big for you, but they're clean."

"Don't you need them?"

He laughed. "Not to be gross, Haley, but I've been on patrol for five days already. There isn't enough real estate in this pack to bring five changes of clothes. When you're out on the trail, you keep wearing the same things until they become unwearable. And *your* socks are unwearable."

He'd been using the same pair of socks for five days? Her nose started to crinkle, until she realized exactly what he was offering her. "Wait, these are your only other pair? Don't you want them?" She held them out, but he pushed them back.

"I want *you* to wear them."

After peeling off her pair, she placed the bandages on her heels and slipped her feet into his socks. Thick, plush wool wrapped around her feet in a moment of pure comfort, like curling up in her favorite chair at home. His down sleeping bag was even better—soft and cozy, with an appealing woodsy scent that reminded her of… well, of *him*. Despite the hard ground, she felt comfortable for the first time all day. A little sigh escaped her lips, and Ezra smiled. The way the skin crinkled around his eyes—like he thought she was cute—made her heart do funny little flips.

Nonsense. He probably smiled at everyone that way.

It was strange, though—how uncomfortable, even downright miserable this entire situation was, and here a virtual stranger was going out of his way to provide for her. Somehow, he didn't feel like a stranger anymore, not after everything they'd been through.

It didn't seem possible that less than twenty-four hours had passed since she'd stumbled across Chris stealing those plans and had to run for her life. Worst day ever. And yet here was Ezra, almost as if he'd been sent by God to help her during this time when she couldn't make it on her own. Guilt lanced through her insides for the things she'd said to him earlier.

"Ezra?"

"Yeah?" He didn't look up from the cookstove, where he was shutting the burner off.

"I'm sorry. About earlier. I shouldn't have pushed you or said that stuff." So much for that image of having it all together. But apologizing was the right thing to do.

He glanced at her, his expression thoughtful, but then he shrugged and turned back to the stove. "It's okay. I'm sorry too. It's been a challenging day for both of us."

The two food bags sat beside the cooking pot, their tops ripped off, and he lifted the pot and poured water directly into the pouches. The instant scent of spicy Tex-Mex meat and beans made her mouth water. He stuck a spoon in each bag and then sat beside her, holding one out. "Dinner's ready. Just stir it up a bit first."

She accepted it gratefully, barely waiting for him to finish saying a blessing on the meal before scooping it out. The rehydrated meat and beans looked like mush on the spoon, but she blew on it and stuffed it into her mouth anyway.

"This is actually really good," she mumbled between bites. "Though I feel like an astronaut."

"Sorry there isn't any freeze-dried ice cream for dessert."

For a moment their earlier argument seemed like it'd never happened. Ezra wasn't like any other man she'd spent time with, and she had to admit, she liked him. *Really* liked him.

While they ate, he told her about the park, its history and geography, its wildlife. How closed up it was in winter because of all the snow. She barely noticed how dark it'd gotten until after he'd cleaned and stowed the cooking equipment, hung his pack from a high branch to keep it away from animals and sat down beside her again.

"Look," he said, pointing up above them. The clearing was big enough to leave a small gap between the trees far overhead. Stars were coming out, little blinking lights glowing against a velvet black sky. "There's no light pollution out here, so you can see all of them."

Her mouth formed into an "O" as she watched. Night descended rapidly, bringing with it a sharp chill in the air, so she pulled his sleeping bag tightly around her. A sudden streak overhead made her sit up straighter. "Look, a shooting star!"

"Yeah. Gorgeous, isn't it? You can see the northern lights sometimes too, but not usually until later in the summer."

She craned her head back, wishing there weren't so many trees. At home, her condo was downtown in one of the new skyscrapers, which meant she never saw anything beyond the moon. Maybe the Big Dipper if it was an especially dark night. She wasn't aware how close she'd leaned to Ezra until her shoulder accidentally bumped into his.

Heat coursed through her cheeks. "Oh, sorry."

"It's okay." He kept his arms locked around his legs, his knees propped up in a mirror of how she was sitting, and for a second, she wished he'd slide one of those arms around her and tuck her in close to his side.

Then she shook off the thought. Ridiculous.

"Well, you'd better try to get a little sleep," he said. "You can stretch out right here on the tarp."

Alarm shot through her body in a flash of panic. "Where are you going?"

His easygoing laugh drifted through the darkness. "Nowhere, don't worry. I'll sit over here and keep watch."

She laid down on the tarp, pulling the mummy-style bag up and around her head, burrowing in deep. The camera was annoying, but she wasn't about to leave it lying on the ground, so she nestled it against her stomach. A yawn slipped out. "Won't you get tired?"

"I'll be okay. Go to sleep now, Haley."

He was moving around, doing something with the backpack, but the haze of exhaustion made it hard for her to pay attention. She'd barely been holding sleep at bay, and now, with a full stomach and the warm, coziness of the bag, she drifted into a sleep far more comfortable than should've been possible for someone in so much trouble.

Ezra thanked the Lord for the hundredth time as he and Haley trudged down the path the next day. Haley had gotten a solid six hours of sleep, and they'd packed up the gear and worked their way back to the trail at dawn without any sign of their pursuers. All of that was a win in his mind.

The first hints of golden daylight peaked up over the mountains in the east, and the fading stars overhead promised a clear sky. One long day to the trailhead. They just might make it. *Please, Lord.*

The day grew warm where the sun penetrated the trees, but the air stayed cool in the shade. The scent of damp earth and moss and decaying leaves wrapped around them, familiar and pleasant. Haley was so tired there were moments Ezra had to take her by the hand and nearly drag her forward.

They only paused a few times for a brief rest or to refill the water bottles. By late afternoon, they'd eaten the last of his protein bars and now had to hike the rest of the way out on empty stomachs. There was no way he'd risk stopping long enough to set up the camp stove and cook a meal.

It was nearing sunset by the time the end of the trail was in sight. Haley had been struggling for the last couple of miles, badly enough that Ezra had resorted to offering rest breaks far more frequently than he wanted. At first, she shook them off and kept pressing on in dogged silence, but before long she would slump down against the first mossy trunk he pointed at.

Now, with only a short distance to go, they sat on a fallen trunk with the creek at their backs. Haley's head was tilted back against a tree, her eyes closed. Concern lanced through his insides, mingled with a healthy dose of impatience. Given her job and what he knew of her lifestyle, she probably wasn't used to this level of exertion. Definitely not this type of stress. He needed to get her back to a safe place to warm up and rest.

"Ready yet?" he prodded.

A snore was the only answer.

Great. He shook her gently. "Haley, you can't sleep yet. We've got to—"

He cut off at a soft sound interrupting the rustling of the wind in the leaves. A snuffling, grunting sound. A dark shape lumbered around a bend in the trail not fifteen feet ahead. Too massive to be a man, it hunched down on all fours in the center of the trail. Even in the fading light the distinctive hunch between its shoulders was clearly visible.

A grizzly bear.

Ezra's chest tightened and he nudged Haley, whispering her name. She jerked awake, gasping in a sharp breath and then going silent. The bear hadn't seen them yet—it was nosing around in the brush, probably looking for berries. Even though it would slow them down, they might be able to slip off the path again and give the animal a wide berth. Most bears weren't looking for an encounter with anyone.

But if it was protecting its territory, or a mother with young...

His blood froze as another, smaller dark shape trundled out of the woods, then a second. Two cubs. Exactly why this national park existed, to protect these God-created, wild animals. But he could've asked for better timing to see them up close.

"What do we do?" Haley's voice was a thready whisper.

"Whatever happens, don't run. We'll have to go around." He pointed into the thick woods off the trail. "That way. Now stand up, nice and slow."

As she did, the mother bear stiffened, lifting her head from the ground. She stared in their direction, two small, dark eyes gleaming in the dying light. Ezra held his breath, his hand inching toward the can of bear spray hanging from his utility belt, waiting to see whether she would ignore them.

Beside him, Haley let out a cross between a shriek and a gasp as the bear rose on her hind legs.

"Don't run," he ordered again, keeping his voice low. He unhooked the bear spray and held it out in front of them.

The bear growled. Ezra kept the bear spray up, at the ready, as he pushed Haley backward with his other arm.

"We're going to back up until she's out of sight, got it? But keep facing forward."

"Okay."

Together, one slow step at a time, they edged away

from the bear until they'd crossed the trail and entered the shadow of the woods. Ezra hesitated a heartbeat, watching as the bear dropped down on all fours. But instead of charging, she turned back to her cubs and the berry bush that had initially claimed her attention. A few steps more into the undergrowth, and she was lost from sight.

Next to him, Haley wobbled and grabbed his arm. "I'm sorry," she whispered, "I just… I…"

Without thinking, he slid his arms around her back and tucked her close against him. Her hands trembled against his chest, but she relaxed as he murmured, "It's okay. That was close. You have every reason to feel scared."

When she glanced up at him, her eyes glistened. She blinked a few times, then slowly pushed herself loose. His arms felt disconcertingly empty. "Thanks."

They gave the bears a wide berth, stepping back out on the trail thirty minutes later, close enough to the trailhead that he could see asphalt through the trees at the end. "Look, almost there!"

Haley nodded wearily, then paused. Listening.

His breath caught as he heard it too. The crackling static of a radio, coming from behind them up the trail.

It *could* be another backcountry ranger, searching for them since he'd missed the helicopter…

But not speaking Russian.

He exchanged a glance with Haley, holding a finger to his lips as he waved her forward and picked up his pace. He'd heard neither gunshots nor screaming, which hopefully meant the grizzlies had moved on, but once the men rounded the bend in the trail, they'd have clean shots at Ezra and Haley.

What was the range on an AK-47 anyway?

They hastened up the path, trying to balance speed with stealth to avoid notice. Any second now it wouldn't matter.

Shouts rang out behind them but that was definitely blacktop up ahead. "Run!" Ezra urged, all but shoving Haley in front of him. They sprinted up the path, feet pounding, debris flying.

A sharp crack rent the air, shattering a tree trunk not far behind and making Haley scream. More bullets bit into the ground and trees nearby, spraying them with dirt and wood chips. His legs burned with the exertion.

"The parking lot!" Haley gasped as they tumbled out of the woods.

Ezra pointed to his vehicle, parked along the forest's edge. "NPS truck."

Their feet pounded the asphalt as they sprinted toward the truck. Haley stopped as they approached the passenger side, but he waved her on.

"Driver's side. Go, go!"

They ducked around the back end of the truck. His fingers shook as he fumbled to get the keys in the lock, then finally the door was open. He shoved Haley inside and climbed in after her. Without being told, she bent low and covered her head and neck.

He slammed the keys into the ignition and cranked the engine just as the men emerged from the trail. Bullets pinged against the side of the truck as he threw the vehicle into Reverse, muttering a quick prayer of thanks that the parking lot was virtually empty.

The truck's tires squealed as he switched the engine to drive and peeled out of the parking lot. In the rear-view mirror, the men slowed, stopping at the edge of the road and lowering their weapons.

He let out a long breath. For the moment, they were safe.

But as the men vanished from view, he caught a glimpse of one of them raising his radio to his mouth. How long would it be before they caught up with him and Haley?

NINE

Haley slumped in the passenger seat of Ezra's truck, barely aware of the miles of curving road drifting past beneath the tires. She couldn't remember when she'd ever felt so exhausted. So empty inside. Except maybe when her mother died. But she'd been much younger then, with fewer cares, and so much less pressure on her shoulders.

Now...now she felt like curling up into a ball in a corner somewhere and crying. Even the feeble prayers she whispered seemed like they were hitting the truck's roof and falling back onto her disheveled, grimy hair.

Fifteen minutes later, the truck rolled to a stop and Haley pried her head off the headrest. They'd pulled into a parking lot with two dozen other cars and trucks near a stretch of identical, tiny bungalows that shouted, "government issue." A larger building at the end of the street reminded her of a cinderblock college dormitory.

"Who lives here again?" she asked. "All the rangers?"

"Only the ones assigned to Newhalem. The park has housing in other areas too. The interpretive and law enforcement rangers are usually always around. It's just the backcountry rangers that take turns going out on patrol. And since most of us are seasonal, this place is pretty empty in winter."

Ezra shut off the engine and climbed out, and Haley followed, taking the big gun that had been resting between her knees during the drive. The street was silent, bathed in darkness except for a blinking fluorescent streetlight and the welcoming glow of porchlights illuminating the front doors.

"Do you think they followed us?" she asked, trailing Ezra across the lot and up a sidewalk toward one of the houses. At least his truck would be hard to identify among the other NPS vehicles unless they inspected for bullet holes.

"Not yet. But with the resources they've got…they'll find us eventually." His jaw muscle tightened as he looked down at his keys. After finding the one he wanted, he twisted it in the lock and popped the door open. "Plus, there's the fact I couldn't call into dispatch after we missed the helicopter. They're expecting to hear from me." He eyed her speculatively for a minute.

Fear tangled its fingers in her ribs. "Can't you let me call Ford first? Before you report back in? I'm only asking for a few minutes, then I'll get out of here and you can tell them—" She cut herself off. Tell them what? He let a wanted criminal go? Had he even reported her in the first place?

He ran a hand over his face, suddenly looking more haggard than she'd seen him yet. Remorse twisted her insides—this wasn't fair, what she was putting him through.

He opened the door and flipped on a light. "Home, sweet home."

She stepped inside, stopping on the small rectangle of linoleum that made up his entryway. The rest of the room was covered with indoor-outdoor carpeting that had seen better days and contained a set of living room furniture that could've come from the nearest rental center. Stark white walls made the place look barely lived in, but on the entertainment unit next to the TV stood a set of photographs she couldn't quite make out from the entryway. At the back of the room, an opening led to a small dining area and kitchen.

After propping the gun against the wall, she stooped to untie her boots and then slid her aching feet out. Ezra closed the door behind them and dropped his backpack to the floor. While he pulled the curtains shut across the front-facing living room window, she drifted over to the TV, trying to look casual as she examined the pictures.

A woman with brown hair curling past her shoulders and a soft, pretty smile. She reminded Haley of the young moms at church—kind and selfless and gentle, always ready to lend a hand in the nursery or mend a scraped knee. Not ambitious and work-obsessed, the way *she* was. The second photograph was of a little girl, barely more than a toddler, with darling chubby cheeks and big, twinkling brown eyes. And in the third picture, the same little girl sat between the woman and Ezra.

His family.

Her mouth went dry, and she swallowed. He didn't wear a ring. Yet their pictures were here, the only indication that anyone even lived in this sterile place. What had happened?

Behind her, he cleared his throat. So much for casual. She opened her mouth to ask about them, but he cut her off.

"Let me show you the bathroom so you can clean up." He didn't make eye contact, turning away to head for a hallway to the right of the entry. Only a few feet down he pushed open a door, revealing a small bathroom with a shower stall, toilet and sink surrounded by a chipped laminate counter. The linoleum floor was peeling up in one corner. When he looked up at her, his cheeks carried a hint of red. "Sorry, I know it's not what you're used to. If I'd known I'd be bringing back a guest, I'd have cleaned a little better."

Compassion flooded through her system. After all they'd been through, he was worried what she'd think about the bathroom? She laid a hand lightly on his arm. "Ezra, it's fine. So long as nobody tries to shoot me and the water's hot, that's all I need."

A reluctant smile cracked his lips. "Let me grab you a towel. Oh, and I probably have a clean shirt." One eyebrow quirked up in question. "If you want it? I'd offer to wash your clothes, but the nearest laundry facility is in the dorm."

"A shirt would be great. Thanks. Can I use your landline too? In case my phone is being traced?"

He disappeared and while she waited, she carefully removed the camera and set it gently on the countertop next to the sink. Then she pulled out her battered cell phone and slipped off her jacket.

The phone appeared dry enough now, but she bit her lip as she pressed the power button. Never had anything sounded better than the cheerful ping of it coming back on. She opened her contacts and pulled up Ford's number as Ezra returned. He set a towel and a folded charcoal-gray T-shirt on the counter, then passed her a cordless phone handset along with a pen and paper.

She quickly jotted down Ford's number and shut the phone back off. It would never even have occurred to her that Chris might be tracing her number if Ezra hadn't said something earlier. Yet another reason to be thankful he was helping her.

He frowned. "You sure you can trust this guy? We could bypass him and go directly to people I know within the police department."

"Ford? Absolutely." The words popped out without hesitation. "He's been my dad's lawyer since before I was born. I appreciate the offer, I do, but…I just don't know if that's safe. Especially with those men still after us. Chris will know right where to find me if I'm in police custody. But as soon as Ford and I can download the evidence, get it to the authorities and show my dad, I'll turn myself in. Promise." Once her father knew the truth and the evidence was safe in the right hands, surely they'd see she was innocent.

He was silent for a long moment. "Fine. But I'm going to get in touch with a friend of mine on the force to see what he knows about your case." The stern expression on his face didn't leave room for argument. Besides, it would be better to know what she was facing.

"Okay, I can agree to that."

"Where are you going to meet this lawyer?"

Good question. She tugged at her lower lip. "What do you think? He's got a plane. What's the closest airstrip? Chelan?"

"No, there's one at Stehekin. We can't drive to it, but we could ride in on horseback. I've got a friend who can hook us up with horses."

She shook her head. "I can't drag you any deeper into this. Isn't there somewhere I can get to on my own?"

"And how exactly are you going to do that? Walk? There's nowhere around here to rent a car, and even if you could, you'd get arrested as soon as anyone heard your name."

"Uber?" Her voice sounded tiny even in her own ears. He had a point.

He raised an eyebrow. "In the national park? Try again. Besides, they're more likely to be monitoring the roads than the trail system. Like it or not, you still need my help."

Trouble was, she *did* like it. More than she cared to admit. After so many years fending for herself, being with Ezra made her feel safe. Even with those guys with guns chasing them. There was a spark between them, probably only because of this shared, wild experience, but it was more than she'd felt with any man, ever. She'd never quite been able to pinpoint why her and Xander's relationship felt off if it was true love, but now it was obvious. Haley hadn't known then what a real connection could feel like. And if she'd been stuck out here with Xander—or any other man, for that matter—she'd already be dead.

The truth needled its way into her tattered heart. Ezra had kept her alive.

Still, it wasn't going to last. She'd be saying goodbye to him soon, and for his sake, the sooner the better. She'd put him in enough danger already. "Won't you get in trouble for not turning me in?"

He let out a long sigh. "Probably. I've got to check back in soon or else more rangers could get tangled up in this mess searching for us. But I'll think of something."

"All right. I'll see if he can meet us in Stehekin. How long will it take to get there?"

"If I can arrange it with my friend, we could drive to his place in the morning and be on the trail within a few hours. We'd have to camp on the trail overnight but then you'd get into town by early afternoon."

"So, two days from now, four o'clock?"

"Yeah." As he nodded, a shadow passed across his face but vanished again almost immediately. Was he thinking the same thing she had only a moment before? That saying goodbye wouldn't be as easy as it should be?

She shook the thought away, her mind catching on something he'd said. "Wait, if it's a town, why can't we drive?"

This time his lips tilted into a grin. "It's only accessible by ferry, float plane, the airstrip or a trail. No road. I'll show you on the map after you clean up."

She shut the door behind him and tapped in Ford's number, holding her breath as the phone rang. What if he was gone, overseas on a trip or something? She hadn't considered that possibility.

But the tension washed out of her chest as the lines connected and he answered. "Ford Anderson. Haley, is that you?"

"Yeah. Yes. This is Haley." The words came out weakly, choked by two days' worth of emotion and trauma. Relief made her knees sag, and she leaned against the bathroom countertop.

"Haley, what a relief. Your father is worried sick. Where are you?" His familiar voice, strong and reassuring, wrapped comfortably around her and removed any doubts that everything would work out. Going to him had been the right call—he'd been at her father's side Haley's whole life.

She spilled out the entire horrible story, absorbing his shock and patiently answering his questions. When the account was done, she added, "But please don't tell Dad yet, Mr. Anderson. Not until we're together and you've seen the video footage. He'll only worry more if he thinks I'm lost in the woods and being hunted like an animal."

"You sure, Haley? He's pretty upset about everything. It might help if he heard your side of the story."

She swallowed, reading between the lines. *Her dad believed Chris.* But who knew what kind of fake evidence Chris had conjured to convince her father of her guilt? Ford's confirmation made her only more determined. "No, I want to wait until we can show him the proof of my innocence and get this evidence safely uploaded to the police. Someone who isn't paid off by Chris," she added. She'd have to ask Ezra who to contact.

He was silent for a moment, long enough that anxiety prickled at the edges of her insides. Then he sighed. "Very well. Tell me where and when to meet you, and I'll be there."

"Stehekin State Airport, 4:00 p.m., two days from now. It's just turf, no tower."

"Got it. And what about the ranger? Is he going to help you get there?"

"Yes. He's going to help." That pesky feeling of warmth surged through her limbs, but she ignored it. Not helpful, not when they'd be going back to normal life like they'd never met.

"Good. Be safe, Haley."

She hung up and set the phone back on the counter, offering up a quick prayer of thanks. Just a couple more days and she'd get this camera safely into Ford's hands and this whole mess would go away.

Then why did this tremor of worry still vibrate through her bones?

An hour later, Ezra rubbed his damp hair with a towel and left the bathroom to find Haley puttering around in his tiny galley kitchen. Dark circles still hovered beneath her eyes, but her cheeks were rosy and clean, and her blond hair curled around her shoulders. She wore the charcoal North Cascades T-shirt he'd given her, along with her jeans, which now bore large wet patches instead of dirt smears.

When she caught him glancing at her legs, she shrugged. "I tried to wash out some of the dirt. It'll have to do."

"Sorry. I wish we could risk the laundromat." But being seen by other rangers would be a bad call at this point. He desperately wanted to notify dispatch that he and Haley were safe, but there would be protocols to follow and questions to answer, and in two shakes she'd be under arrest. Assuming, of course, those men didn't get to her first.

In the end, he'd settled for leaving a voice mail for the chief ranger, who would hear it tomorrow morning when he and Haley were already on the trail to Stehekin.

He pointed at the counter, where she'd set out a canister of instant coffee and a mug. "Isn't it a little late for caffeine?"

"I need a little or I won't stay awake long enough to eat."

Treat Yourself
with 2 Free Books!

Claim up to FOUR NEW BOOKS & TWO MYSTERY GIFTS – absolutely FREE!

Dear Reader,

We both know life can be difficult at times. That's why it's important to treat yourself so you can relax and recharge once in a while.

And I'd like to help you do this by sending you this amazing offer of up to FOUR brand new full length FREE BOOKS that WE pay for.

This is everything I have ready to send to you right now:

Try **Love Inspired® Romance Larger-Print** books and fall in love with inspirational romances that take you on an uplifting journey of faith, forgiveness and hope.

Try **Love Inspired® Suspense Larger-Print** books where courage and optimism unite in stories of faith and love in the face of danger.

Or **TRY BOTH!**

All we ask in return is that you answer 4 simple questions on the attached Treat Yourself survey. You'll get **Two Free Books** and **Two Mystery Gifts** from each series you try, *altogether worth over $20*! Who could pass up a deal like that?

Sincerely,

Pam Powers

Harlequin Reader Service

Treat Yourself to Free Books and Free Gifts.

Answer 4 fun questions and get rewarded.

We love to connect with our readers! Please tell us a little about you...

▶ **DETACH AND MAIL CARD TODAY!** ▶

TREAT YOURSELF • Pick your 2 Free Books...

Yes! Please send me my Free Books from each series I select and Free Mystery Gifts. I understand that I am under no obligation to buy anything, as explained on the back of this card.

Which do you prefer?
- ❏ **Love Inspired® Romance Larger-Print** 122/322 IDL GRDP
- ❏ **Love Inspired® Suspense Larger-Print** 107/307 IDL GRDP
- ❏ **Try Both** 122/322 & 107/307 IDL GRED

FIRST NAME   LAST NAME

ADDRESS

APT.#   CITY

STATE/PROV.   ZIP/POSTAL CODE

EMAIL ❏ Please check this box if you would like to receive newsletters and promotional emails from Harlequin Enterprises ULC and its affiliates. You can unsubscribe anytime.

LI/SLI-520-TY22

"Glad you feel at home enough to help yourself."
It'd been a long time since there'd been a woman in his
kitchen. If he was being honest, it was nice. Really nice.

Her cheeks tinged pink. "Microwave?"

"Nope." He pulled out a saucepan and filled it with
water. "We do things the old-fashioned way around
here." After setting the pan on the stove, he tugged
open the refrigerator door. A slimy bag of carrots, a
gallon of water and a fuzzy block of cheese stared back
at him. He winced. "Sorry, I don't keep much in here
when I'm heading out on the trail."

She glanced over his shoulder, then turned away to
rummage through the cabinets. "Makes sense. Where
do you grocery shop anyway? This place is in the middle of nowhere."

"There's a town with a store about an hour away. We
take turns making trips out there." He pulled open the
freezer and found a bag of frozen kung pao chicken.
"Here, we can heat this up."

"And some ramen noodles." Haley held up a package in each hand, a ridiculous smile plastered across
her face. "Like college all over again."

"At least I've got my own kitchen. The rangers stuck
in the dorm have to share."

"How do people do this job with families?" She tilted
her head, watching him. Like she was hoping for more
information.

Nope. "It would be challenging. Most seasonal rangers are single. We're paid in sunsets, as they say."

They set to work preparing the food. Ezra had to
admit it was far easier to be with her than he would've
guessed two days ago, considering her upbringing and
living standards, and the way she'd acted on the trail

when he first met her. Now she didn't offer a single complaint. Even when she took her first sip of instant coffee, she merely commented on how good the heat felt. It was like he'd gotten beneath the wealthy heiress facade and made it down to the real Haley.

And he liked the real Haley. A lot.

After scooping hot ramen noodles and spicy kung pao onto their plates, they sat at the small dining table at the far end of the kitchen.

"I talked to a friend on the force," he said as he twirled noodles onto his fork. "It's not good right now, Haley."

Her throat bobbed. "I figured. What do they have?"

"They found the murder weapon for the dead security guard in your office. There's video footage of you entering and exiting the building, which coincides with the approximate time of death. But nothing for your floor because someone tampered with all the security cameras."

She passed a hand over her eyes. "Any footage of Chris coming and going?"

He shook his head slowly. "But that doesn't mean he couldn't have had someone hack into the system and delete it. We have your evidence and my testimony about the men chasing us out here. It'll be enough."

"As long as we can get it back in one piece."

"Do you want me to download the files from your SD card to create a backup?" he asked around a mouthful of hot chicken.

"Can you?" She paused with her fork halfway to her mouth. "I didn't think about that, but maybe I could compress the video and email the zip file to Ford. Or one of your friends on the force. Then we wouldn't have to worry about the camera itself anymore."

He frowned. "The internet is terrible out here. It'd never send. But we could make a copy. And keep a backup on my hard drive."

Eating didn't take long, and after cleaning up the kitchen, Haley waited with her camera in the living room while he grabbed his laptop from the bedroom. When he emerged from the hallway, she was staring at the pictures on the TV stand again. One of his hands knotted itself into a fist. There'd be no avoiding a conversation this time.

Especially not with the speculative glance she gave him as soon as he came closer.

He sat down on the sofa, near enough for her to see the laptop easily but keeping a respectful distance. She waited as he opened the computer and pressed the power button, and for a moment he thought he might get away with not saying anything.

"Who are they?" Her gentle, quiet words broke the silence in the room. She tipped her head at the pictures, then watched him, waiting.

A soul-deep sigh slipped out. Might as well just spill it all. He stood, grabbed the family photo and sat back down on the couch. A wave of fresh emotion threatened to choke him, and his hands shook as he looked at them—his wife in her Sunday best and his little girl in the Easter dress she'd loved.

"My wife and daughter." He wasn't sure how he managed to get the words out.

Next to him, Haley's gaze drifted to his left hand. Looking for the ring that should've been there.

That *used* to be there.

He shook his head, fighting to get words out against the thickness in his throat. "They're gone. Three years ago. Sarah took Kaitlyn for ice cream after her first day of preschool. They invited me to come but—" his voice hitched but he kept his focus on the picture, not daring to look at Haley and see the pity on her face "—I was on duty." He paused, struggling to keep the dam he'd so carefully constructed from breaking. When was the last time he'd talked about them?

"What happened?" Haley's soft voice was achingly gentle.

"A guy was on his cell phone. Rear-ended Sarah while she was waiting to turn left into the parking lot. Pushed her car into the oncoming traffic. It was ugly." His voice choked up again, and he swallowed. "She died on the scene. They took Kaitlyn to the hospital but…" Pressure built inside his head, behind his sinuses, and the back of his esophagus burned. He'd held Kaitlyn's little hand, wrapped tightly in his own, as they wheeled her into surgery.

I love you, sweetheart, so much. I'm praying for you.

She'd smiled at him. Then looked past him, like she was seeing beyond to a place he couldn't go. Not yet. Her face had shone as her eyelids drifted shut.

"She…she didn't make it out of surgery." His eyes burned, coating over with a film of tears, and he blinked it away. The last thing he needed to do was break down in front of Haley. He could deal with it later when they didn't have to get her to safety.

"Oh, Ezra. I'm so sorry." Her words wrapped around his heart like a soft blanket. But the usual fear he felt whenever someone found out pricked at him too. Haley was a believer—would she offer the same trite reassurances of God's good plan?

She sat in silence for a long moment, looking at the picture cradled in his hands. "She was beautiful. They both were."

When he finally summoned the courage to look up at her, a sheen of moisture glistened in her eyes and the tip of her nose had turned red. Then he remembered what she'd said on the trail about her mother dying when she was young.

She knew.

Haley knew what it was like, losing somebody that should've had years and years more to spend with you. How the loss could go on and on without end because every single time you wanted to touch or see or talk to that person, you had to be reminded afresh that they were gone. An open wound that felt like it would never heal.

"Thank you." He nearly choked on the words, and before he quite knew what had happened, Haley wrapped both arms around him. He leaned into her touch, letting her comfort him in a way nobody had for three years. "It's hard," he whispered into her shoulder.

"I still miss my mom, every single day." Her voice had grown thick. "I can only imagine how tough this must be for you. Thank you for sharing it with me."

After a long moment, she released him and he pulled back, stopping with their faces inches apart. Her blue eyes were still glossy with the empathy of grief, no less beautiful for the dark shadows beneath them. A strand of silky blond hair had escaped from behind her shoulder and rested against her cheek, and before he thought about what he was doing, he lifted a finger and brushed it back.

Something shifted in her eyes, the grief flitting away as they widened in a rare glimpse of openness. That odd combination of strength and vulnerability, self-assurance mingled with fleeting moments of fragility, called to him like a complex piece of music he couldn't quite understand. But he wanted to—oh, how he wanted to. His fingers rested against the soft skin of her cheek and his gaze dropped to her lips.

He moved closer, warily, not completely sure what he was thinking, but then the picture of his family started to slide from his lap. With a start, he jerked back awkwardly and fumbled to catch it before it plunged to the floor. Heat burned up the back of his neck.

What was *wrong* with him? How could he go from talking about Sarah and Kaitlyn to nearly kissing another woman mere seconds later? Especially Haley Whitcombe, who was more or less the opposite of Sarah? Wanted for criminal charges—granted, she'd be able to clear those up—but more so, the fame, the obsession with work, the rich lifestyle... Those weren't the things he and Sarah had been about. They'd invested in a quiet life, family, their church community.

Deep down, he knew he wasn't being fair to Haley, but the guilt of his betrayal stung like a spider bite and overwhelmed every other feeling. He climbed to his feet and gently set the frame back on top of the TV, then cleared his throat. "Let's get those files downloaded."

On the couch, Haley shifted back against the armrest and smoothed her hair behind her ears with brisk movements. From the way her cheeks had blanched, she felt just as shocked as he did. "Yes, of course." She busied herself extracting the SD card from the camera.

Where had all these unwanted feelings come from? It *had* to be the result of their intense situation, nothing more. He kept a safe distance as he sat down again and took the small card from her, being careful not to let their fingers touch.

Two more days, and he could hand her off to her father's friend and get back to his normal life full of blessed solitude. Two days.

But why did being alone suddenly sound so...*lonely*?

TEN

Haley tried to focus on the computer screen as Ezra inserted the SD card into his laptop, but her mind wouldn't cooperate.

What had just happened? How had a moment of comfort transitioned so quickly into a near *kiss*?

Or maybe that was all in her head. Maybe he hadn't been gazing at her mouth, leaning in closer. It'd been ages since a man had kissed her—not since Xander—and she'd never had this cascade of butterflies in her stomach with him. Kissing him always felt like what couples were expected to do. Part of the deal.

But kissing somebody you just met a few days ago, while on the run for a crime you didn't commit? Stuff like that happened in movies, not real life. Here in the real world, people had commitments they couldn't just ignore. Hurts they couldn't move on from at the drop of a hat. She thought of the photograph Ezra had replaced on the TV stand.

Neither of them was looking for a relationship. *If* anything had been about to happen, it was a moment of weakness brought on by the stress of the situation. Nothing deeper.

"Haley?" His voice broke into her thoughts, and she realized she'd missed most of what he was saying.

She cleared her throat. "What?"

"Which files?"

"All of them." She pointed at the tiny icons on the screen. "See these? They're pictures of plans for one of our engine prototypes. My father always keeps hard copies to be safe, locked up in a storage room attached to his office. He doesn't digitize anything until it's ready for production."

"Then how did this guy get to the plans to take pictures?"

"Chris? He's like Dad's right-hand man, second only to me." She still had a hard time wrapping her mind around his betrayal, even with firsthand evidence. "He's got a key to every door in the office."

Ezra's eyebrows raised. "Oh. That's a big deal. Why did he kill the guard?"

The dead man's contorted face flashed into her mind and she grimaced. So awful. "My guess is, he asked Chris one too many questions. Maybe even wanted clearance from my father. Taking pictures of those plans in the middle of the night would look weird, even for me or Chris."

"Okay, but why? Why steal anything if he's practically second in charge? Seems like a pretty good gig already, if you ask me."

Her shoulders slumped, and she dragged her hands through her hair. "My dad just announced I'd be his replacement as CEO. Some of the board members thought it was a given, but others were rooting for Chris. He's got a brilliant head for business, more so than me." Maybe that admission should've cost more, but after how hard she worked to act like she belonged in management, it felt good to admit the truth. "The science is my thing, not the business side. I always wanted to go to grad school and become a project manager for R&D, but Dad… Anyway, last year Chris and his contingent of supporters advocated we take a deal from this Swiss company, but my father was convinced the company was a facade for the Russian government, so he turned it down. It was for a lot of money—probably made the best business sense—but he felt it wasn't patriotic. Or even ethical, for that matter."

"Russian, huh? Up in the glacial valley, the blond one spoke with a Russian accent."

"Yeah, I noticed. It doesn't necessarily mean anything, but I'm wondering if Chris decided to go behind our backs and make the deal after he got passed over. Either out of spite, or because he's planning on retiring early on his earnings."

Ezra glared at the laptop as he copied the files onto his hard drive. "The fact he's trying to blame you makes it sound like spite."

"But it's also the only other logical explanation, unfortunately. Nobody else has the access we do. And if I snuck in to steal plans and got caught, is it a stretch that I'd kill the guard too?" She sighed.

"I wonder what motive he concocted. Why would you need to steal?"

"Greed? Dissatisfaction with my dad's decisions? Who knows? I'll find out soon enough." The thought twinged painfully. Soon she'd be back in Seattle, and even with Ford at her side, there'd be an awful mess to untangle. It made her appreciate the glorious simplicity of being out here in the mountains, far away from the chaos of her life.

"Okay, it's all on my hard drive. I'm going to make a backup on this memory stick." He waved a small black flash drive, then stuck it into the USB port. When the transfer was complete, he ejected both the flash drive and the SD card, holding them out to her.

She accepted the SD card, sliding it back into the camera. Maybe it'd be more practical to carry it in her clothing, but it seemed safer inside the camera. Less chance it would fall out of her pocket or wash away in another stream. But the flash drive—he should hold onto that in case somebody managed to catch her. Then their backup would be safe.

"You keep the flash drive for me." She paused, biting her lip as she considered what she was truly asking. He'd already put his life in danger multiple times, and now, carrying this evidence…storing it on his laptop… It was risky. "Unless you don't want to."

In answer, he stowed it in the pocket of his gray cargo pants. He'd swapped out his button-down NPS uniform shirt for a plain, dark green T-shirt, his official badge no longer in sight. Was it to avoid notice in case their pursuers caught up with them? Or because by helping her, he'd basically gone rogue?

He was putting both his job and his life on the line for her. Discomfort twisted her insides—possibly guilt, but more likely something else that almost felt worse. Shame. How had her life gotten so broken, even though she'd been trying to do everything right?

"God doesn't make sense sometimes," she muttered. Warmth invaded her cheeks as he looked at her, surprise flickering across his features, and she realized she'd said it aloud.

"No, He doesn't. Not this side of heaven." A ghost of a smile flitted across his face, creating the humor lines that made him so attractive. "I guess it's that whole He's-infinite-we're-finite thing."

She couldn't help smiling back. Somehow everything felt lighter, easier, with Ezra. "Yeah, you might be right about that."

He closed the laptop. "Let me return this and grab you some blankets. Hopefully we can get some sleep and then start for Rob's before dawn. He's expecting us at 7:30 a.m."

A few minutes later, he returned with a pillow and a stack of downy-soft microfiber fleece blankets. She plumped the pillow and snuggled underneath the blankets. The camera rested right in front of her on the coffee table, the first thing she'd see when she woke. "Thanks," she mumbled, her eyelids drifting shut as she pulled the blankets up to her chin. "These are super cozy."

It felt like home, being with him.

No, she hadn't meant that. Her brain was scrambled, falling asleep.

His low, soft voice drifted across her thoughts. "You're welcome. Sleep well, Haley."

Despite his exhaustion, Ezra tossed and turned in his bed. Two nights in a row now he'd "tucked" that woman in, and somewhere along the way taking care of her had shifted from being a burden to being something he actually enjoyed. Maybe even *wanted* to do. And yet guilt prickled his insides—how could he forget Sarah so easily? Disregard her and their daughter and the life they'd shared? Was three years of mourning long enough?

But he hadn't really mourned, had he? Every time the painful chasm of grief opened, he snapped it shut. Wasn't that the real reason he avoided his sister? Or talking about his loss? He reached for the crumpled photo on his nightstand, the one he carried on every patrol, and stared at the faces he'd never see again in this lifetime, barely visible in the blue glow of his alarm clock. What would Sarah want for him?

Foolishness. It didn't matter what she would say, because there was no future for him and Haley, no matter how much he might be drawn to her. She had her own life—and her own problems—to get back to in Seattle. There was only so much he could do to help and then they'd go their separate ways.

If that thought didn't hurt so much, maybe he'd be able to fall asleep.

After a long time, he glanced at the clock. 3:30 a.m. He must've slept, or at least dozed. The house was silent, except for a soft scratching noise coming from the living room, almost like metal on metal.

Haley? She should be sound asleep.

All the hairs stood on his neck as he bolted upright. No, that was the sound of someone trying to pick a door lock.

He swiveled out of bed, grabbed his gun from the nightstand and made sure it was loaded. After tucking his utility belt around his waist, he threw on his boots and tiptoed out to the living room. If they were bothering to pick the lock rather than shoot the door open, that meant they assumed he and Haley were still asleep. Better to let them keep thinking that.

Haley *was* asleep, softly illuminated by the street-light shining in through the gap between the curtains. She lay curled on her side, his blankets wrapped under her chin like she didn't have a care in the world. Too bad their lives were on the line yet again.

"Psst, Haley," he hissed, shaking her gently.

She jerked upright, breathing heavily as she glanced around the room, ready for danger. He squeezed her arm softly, then pointed toward the front door where the scratching continued.

She froze, her gaze darting to the door, then back to his face.

He tipped his head toward the kitchen. "Back door."

Haley slipped on her jacket, put the camera strap over her shoulder and stood, then hesitated, glancing at the entryway. Her boots—they were next to the front door. Before he could say anything, she skirted the edge of the couch and bolted for the kitchen in her socks.

They'd barely made it into the next room, behind the relative safety of the wall of kitchen cabinets, before the front door swung open with a soft creak. Heavy boots thudded into the entryway, and a rattling, metallic sound suggested somebody had found the AK-47 Haley had left propped up next to the door.

No time to waste. Ezra grabbed her hand and pulled her through the narrow kitchen to the other end, where a door with a glass window led outside. He and the other rangers had always joked about how bungalows this small hardly needed a second door, but now he was grateful. *Thank You, God, for building codes.*

After flipping the lock back, he swung the door

open. Hopefully nobody would be waiting outside. Muffled voices spoke inside the living room, but he couldn't make out what they were saying. The soft thump of boots indicated they were moving farther in to search, and a beam of light flickered across the table at the other end of the kitchen.

He stuck his head out, relieved to see nothing but empty, quiet night, then slipped all the way out, holding the door open for Haley. As he pulled it shut behind her, a flashlight beam whipped down the length of the kitchen and he ducked, dropping into a crouch. The light sifted through the thin curtain covering the glass.

Haley stood off to one side, clutching her camera, and he took her hand and dragged her behind the bungalow. On the other side of the small lawn loomed a dark mass of woods. They barely made it into the cover of the trees before a sharp *thunk* came from the house, followed by angry, indiscernible voices.

"Come on!" Ezra pulled Haley after him as he dashed between the trees in the darkness. The moon had risen, casting a soft, silvery glow through gaps in the canopy above, and providing much-needed light to help them avoid stumbling. But if *they* could see, their pursuers would be able to also. "Guess they figured out we're not there."

"Do you think—" she paused, gasping for air "—they found your laptop?"

"If so, it can't be helped. At least we have the flash drive."

"Where are we going? How can we reach your friend's house now?"

He pointed ahead to where streetlights peeked out

from between the trees. "Park headquarters. I've got my keys. We can get a different vehicle."

They burst out from the forest, racing across a clearing and over the empty parking lot, feet pounding on asphalt. The building was dark except for the orange glow of the exterior lights. It wouldn't stay that way for long, though, if any of his neighbors woke up and notified security. He led Haley around front, stopping only long enough to cram his key into the lock and wrench the door open.

The interior was quiet and dark, and he resisted the urge to flip on the lights, instead feeling his way by instinct. Holding Haley's hand, he guided her to the desk where they kept the keys for the vehicles. Nearly all of them had been assigned to rangers, but there were always a couple of backups. He grabbed a set of keys and they retreated out the front door, locking it behind them.

"This way," he whispered, waving toward the other side of the building where two NPS trucks were parked. Checking the tag on the keys, he found the right one, unlocked the passenger door for Haley and then climbed in behind the wheel.

No one had appeared. Yet. But the tension didn't ease in his body even as he cranked the engine and threw the truck into Reverse, keeping the headlights off.

They still had a long way to go to get Haley to her rendezvous in Stehekin, and now they had nothing but the evidence. No equipment. No food or supplies. No radio. No wallet with a driver's license. Haley didn't even have shoes.

He turned onto the main road and headed west toward his friend Rob's, driving at a crawl until it felt safe to switch the headlights on. Hopefully Rob would be able to help with some of their needed supplies. As he passed the turnoff for the ranger bungalows, he caught a glimpse of the residential parking lot. A black SUV sat in one of the spots. That definitely hadn't been there last night. The men were apparently still pursuing on foot, but it was only a matter of time before they realized he and Haley had slipped away.

Maybe only minutes, even. When they'd made it a few miles past the ranger housing, he flipped on the headlights and pressed the accelerator, trying to gain as much distance as possible. Would it be enough?

ELEVEN

The truck sped around one bend after another, the headlights illuminating only a short distance into the inky darkness ahead. Haley's feet throbbed, both from yesterday's blisters and tonight's race through the woods. Every time she hunched over to pick another pine needle out of her sock, the truck would lurch sideways as it went around a curve in the road. She was going to need a car-sickness bag before long.

"Sorry," Ezra muttered as they swerved around another turn. "This road is really beautiful in the day."

"I keep hearing how relaxing and beautiful this park is, but after my experience, I'm pretty sure the brochure was lying," she deadpanned.

He rewarded her with a warm laugh, the kind that made her insides feel squishy and her heart feel safe. What if they kept in touch during the off-season when he was back in Seattle?

But even as the question crossed her mind, she knew there were too many obstacles in the way to make a casual friendship worth maintaining, especially when deep down she'd always be hoping for more. They both seemed like the all-or-nothing type when it came to relationships. Not to mention, he hadn't gotten over his wife and she'd sworn off romance after Xander, so clearly, she needed to stop these uninvited thoughts about Ezra before she said—or did—something she'd regret.

It was okay to like and respect him. And she was incredibly grateful he'd kept her alive. But to consider more between them? That was out.

The thought hurt.

"You okay?" Ezra asked. "How are your feet?"

"Full of pine needles, but I'll be all right. Do you think we can get some boots somewhere?"

"I'm hoping Rob might have a spare pair. As you might have gathered, there aren't exactly any stores out here."

She turned around in her seat, glancing behind them through the rear window at the dark road. "Not that it would be safe to stop even if there were."

Mercifully no headlights appeared behind them. An hour later they pulled off onto a bumpy dirt road leading into even blacker darkness. Her tailbone protested as the truck jostled and bounced over ruts in the road. Good thing Ezra knew where he was going because *she* couldn't see a thing.

A split rail fence appeared along one side of the road, and after a few minutes, Ezra rolled to a stop in front of a two-story house with a wide front porch. He flipped off the headlights and killed the ignition. "We're here two hours earlier than I intended, so I might have to wake Rob up."

They climbed out of the truck and shut the doors, then walked up the front steps to the porch. Well, Ezra walked, *she* hobbled. He rapped softly on the door, keeping his fist upraised, but a moment later the door swung open.

The man on the other side was dressed in flannel pajama pants, a white T-shirt and a long fleece bathrobe. His gray hair stuck up at odd angles, and his mouth was stretched into a wide grin beneath a pair of black-framed eyeglasses.

"Ezra, Haley! Come in, come in!" He opened the door wider, extending an arm to invite them inside. "I wasn't expecting ya'll till seven thirty, but you're welcome to tuck into a little breakfast with us. Nina's just fryin' up the bacon." With a wink at Haley, he added, "We get an early start around here."

A homey smell of salty, fried meat greeted Haley's nostrils as she followed Ezra into the entryway. Her stomach rumbled in response. A braided rug laid out over gorgeous wide-plank wood floors greeted her tender feet.

After their host had closed the door, Ezra clapped him on the shoulder and turned to her. "Haley, this is Rob Callahan. Rob, this is Haley."

Rob extended his hand and shook hers. Ezra hadn't offered her last name—would Rob recognize her? But the expression on the older man's face showed no flicker of recognition, and he said heartily, "Welcome! I don't know how much Ezra told you, but we run an outfitters business here in the national park and forest, mainly specializing in trail rides. Good time for you two though, because I've got a break between groups for a couple of days."

A woman appeared at the end of a hallway running next to a staircase leading to the second floor. Light from the room behind her—presumably the kitchen—

framed her where she stood in the doorway, wiping her hands on a towel. "What's the holdup out here, Rob Callahan? You gonna make those poor folks stand in the entryway all morning, while the food gets cold?"

Rob laughed, belly deep. "Hold your horses, we're coming." When they reached her, he swooped her up into a hug, lifting her off the ground, then set her down and kissed her cheek. "This is my better half, Nina. She cooks up a mean breakfast. Don't matter if it's here in the kitchen or on the trail."

"Knock it off, you." She swatted him with the towel, but laughter danced in the crinkles around her eyes. Her salt-and-pepper hair had more black in it than Rob's solid gray, and she moved with the vitality and grace of someone who loved life.

The kitchen matched what Haley had seen of the house—exposed rafters on the vaulted ceiling, rich cherry cabinets with a granite countertop, and the same wide-plank floors. A big farmhouse table stretched away from the kitchen toward a stone fireplace at the other end of the space, surrounded by tall windows. It was still dark outside, but she imagined the view must be spectacular.

In a matter of minutes, Rob and Nina had set two more places at the table. Haley and Ezra helped carry over the food, and then the two of them took seats opposite their hosts. The scents of steaming scrambled eggs, roasted potatoes and sizzling bacon were enough to make her mouth water. How many days had it been since she'd eaten something that didn't come out of a package or need to be reconstituted with water?

Even more surprising, how long had it been since she'd had this big of an appetite?

Her fingers itched to reach for the nearest serving spoon, but Rob held out his hands. "I know Ezra won't mind if we say grace. You all right with that, Haley?"

She smiled. How delightful to meet more believers. "That would be wonderful."

Nina's outstretched hand waited on the table, and Haley took it. She turned to Ezra. Something flickered in his gaze as he held out his hand. It shouldn't be awkward—they'd held hands dozens of times already in their madcap dashes through the woods—but this was the first time she noticed how neatly hers fit inside his. How he cradled her fingers delicately despite so much rough strength. How the contact shot a flash of warmth up her arm.

When the prayer ended, she thought for sure he took longer than necessary to let go, like he didn't want the contact to end, either. But he kept his focus on their hosts as he thanked them again for their generosity.

She accepted the steaming coffeepot from Nina and poured a cup, taking a deep breath of the strong, rich scent. Whatever Nina had brewed would clearly taste a thousand times better than Ezra's instant coffee. "Do you eat such a big breakfast every day?" she asked.

"Only on trail days." Rob scooped eggs onto his plate. "We get an early start every day because of the horses, but when we're leading groups out, we want to start strong."

"Plus Rob mentioned ya'll were coming this morning," Nina added. "I figured you might be hungry, so leftovers wouldn't hurt."

Ezra's smile vanished as he speared a piece of potato on his plate. "Rob, you remember what we talked about last night?"

The older man sobered. "They still after you? Is that why you're here early?"

He nodded, and Haley's stomach clenched around her half-eaten breakfast as the familiar stress bubbled up again. So much for her appetite. How much had he told Rob? She glanced at him, and he met her gaze, shaking his head ever so slightly.

"Found us at my house in the middle of the night, so we escaped and drove here. We weren't followed, but there's always the chance they'll somehow make the connection."

Rob took a sip of coffee, his eyes meeting his wife's over the rim of the mug. "We knew what we were taking on when we offered to help, even though you can't tell us the details."

Nina sat up straighter. "That's right. As the scripture says, a cord of three strands isn't easily broken. True friends help each other in times of need."

Her words were like a balm to Haley's soul. She took a sip of her coffee, letting the warmth seep down deep into her insides until she felt a measure of peace. Behind Nina, outside one of the big picture windows, purple and orange streaks lit up the sky to the east above a dark profile of rugged mountains. More words from the Bible, probably remembered from a Sunday school class long ago, came to mind.

His mercies are new every morning.

Maybe she'd been thinking about it all wrong—maybe His grace *wasn't* something she could earn, but something He freely bestowed, like this beautiful sunrise painted across the mountains. A thirst burned inside her to experience more of God's grace, more of His beauty. More of who He was. She'd pushed knowing

Him to the edges of her life for a long time now, focusing instead on doing all the right things and trying to live up to the standards she'd set for herself. She'd always assumed that was what God wanted too—for her to be the best—but maybe what He really wanted was for her to just...*be*. In a relationship with Him.

The peace that flooded her soul surpassed the warmth of the coffee and even Nina's words, and she blinked back tears.

"Well, thank you, Nina," Ezra said, and when Haley dared a glance at him, he slipped his hand beneath the table and gave hers a squeeze.

Heat crept up the back of her neck, but she squeezed back before withdrawing her hand under the pretense of sipping more coffee. Had he seen her little spiritual epiphany playing out across her face? She usually did a better job guarding her emotions, but this ordeal *had* pushed her nearly to the breaking point. Thankfully it was almost over.

Most of the serving dishes were empty by the time Rob dropped his napkin on his plate, kissed his wife on the cheek and stood. "Ezra, we'd best find you some gear and get the horses loaded into the trailer. The earlier you can start, the better."

"I'll help Nina clear the dishes." Haley stole the plate out of Ezra's hand.

But Nina shook her head, tsk-tsking as she took the plate from Haley. "You, young lady, are going to lie down on the sofa in the living room. You look like you haven't slept in weeks. Like you haven't been fed, either, up until this mornin'." She cast a disapproving eye over Haley's long, lean limbs. "And I'll see if I can rustle up a spare pair of boots."

Haley wanted to object, but her body felt so heavy, it was easier to let Ezra lead her into the living room. The plush sofa, with its Southwestern-style throw pillows, enveloped her as she sank onto it. Ezra cast a crooked smile at her, then followed Rob out the front door. In a matter of minutes, she was asleep.

The horses were loaded into the trailer, Rob had packed two saddlebags with food and gear to get them to Stehekin, and Nina had even scrounged up a pair of boots that were hopefully in Haley's size. Now all Ezra had to do was wake Haley up.

Easier said than done. He wasn't sure he'd ever seen her look as content, as at peace, as she did right now, passed out on the Callahans' sofa. But the sun was rising, soon to crest the mountain range to the east, and they needed to get out on the trail. There was no reason to believe the men had tracked them this far or would know they were heading for Stehekin, but they couldn't be too cautious.

The urge to kiss her forehead swept over him out of nowhere, but he shook it off and instead called her name. These ridiculous feelings that kept popping up needed to be ignored. By tomorrow she'd be gone and things could go back to the way they were supposed to be.

She yawned and stretched blearily, then sat up. "Time to go?"

"Yeah. Everything's ready. Rob's going to drive us to the trailhead and help us get unloaded. Here—" he held out the pair of boots Nina had found "—try these on."

After slipping her feet into the boots, she stood, testing the fit. "They're a little snug, but they'll work. A

whole lot better than bare feet." She offered him a wry
smile.

A few minutes later, they stood on the front porch to
say goodbye to Nina. Early-morning sunlight streamed
around the house, casting a soft, yellow glow on the surrounding woods and fields and turning the dewdrops
into glittering diamonds. Nina gave Haley a hug, then
turned to Ezra. After hugging him, she pressed a kiss
to his cheek.

"You take care of her, you hear? She's a treasure,"
she said softly.

"I will." He stole a glance at Haley to see if she'd heard
Nina's words, but she was already traipsing down the
steps toward the truck and attached horse trailer. "I
know she is."

But she wasn't meant for someone broken like him.
She needed a man who could offer his whole heart, not
one whose heart was still shattered from grief. There'd
been something cathartic about sharing Sarah and Kaitlyn with Haley, though—like he had held out *his* great-
est treasures and Haley had admired and understood.
Now that he thought about it, today was the first day
in a long time where the old grief hadn't burned quite
so painfully. More of a dull ache than a sharp sting he
had to consciously ignore.

He followed her to Rob's truck, an extended cab with
double wheels at the back to help it tow the heavy horse
trailer up steep mountain roads. Once they climbed in
and buckled up, Rob guided the vehicle through the
turnaround in front of the house.

"Where's your truck?" Haley asked as they headed
toward the dirt road that would lead them back to the
main road.

"I parked it in Rob's garage. Just in case anybody comes snooping." He glanced back at Nina, waving from the porch, and prayed a silent prayer of protection over her. It had been risky coming here. The last thing he wanted was to put anyone else in harm's way.

But as they slowly bumped and jostled down the main road, he didn't see the black SUV of their pursuers anywhere, nor any evidence they'd been in the area.

An hour later, Rob pulled into the turnout for Bridge Creek. The trailhead was one of the most popular access points for riding or hiking into Stehekin, and several vehicles were parked off to the side, including an NPS truck. Anxiety gripped his chest in a vise. By now the chief ranger had probably heard his voice mail and realized he and Haley were gone again, and Ezra had compounded the situation by "borrowing" another vehicle in the middle of the night without permission. Of course, if the chief sent anyone to check his house, they'd find the door busted open and whatever damage their pursuers had caused. Before long, every ranger in the park would be on high alert.

And then there were innocent hikers out on the trails, and the gunmen tracking him and Haley...

The whole thing was truly a mess. Maybe it would be more prudent to turn Haley over to police custody now, before anyone got hurt. He could handle the arrest himself on the park service's end. But he dismissed the idea as soon as it occurred to him, not only because of how Haley would react to that kind of betrayal, but because they'd be putting themselves back in the path of their pursuers. And with his police badge back in Seattle during his unpaid leave, she'd be out of his hands as soon as park law enforcement turned her over to Seattle PD.

Whatever happened, he had to make sure Haley and her evidence stayed safe. *And* no innocent bystanders got hurt.

Rob led the two horses out of the back of the trailer while he and Haley grabbed the saddlebags. Under Rob's guidance, they strapped the bags behind the saddles, then walked the horses over to the trailhead.

"You ever ridden before, Haley?" the older man asked her.

She stood near the head of the white-and-black appaloosa, reaching out a tentative hand to touch the mare's nose. "Yeah, but it's been years. Like, since middle school summer camp."

"Well, this old girl will be easy for you, won't you, Oreo?" He patted the horse's neck. "She'd know these trails blindfolded. All you got to do is keep a good seat in the saddle and let her do her thing. Let me help you up."

He handed Haley the reins and showed her how to use the stirrup and saddle horn to hoist herself into the saddle. "Ezra knows a thing or two about horses after three summers out here, so you just follow his lead and he'll take care of them when you stop for the night."

"They'll be in good hands, Rob." Ezra mounted his horse, a bay mare with a gleaming mane and tail named Winifred after Rob's maternal grandmother. Winny shook her head, the bit clattering in her teeth, and she let out a little snort like she was anxious to be off.

"Guess you're done with the chitchat, huh, girl?" Rob gave her an affectionate rub on the nose. "Ezra, I'll meet you back here at sunset, day after tomorrow. We'll be praying for you, Haley."

"Thanks, Rob. And tell Nina thank you too." Haley

pressed a hand to her heart. "I hope I can come visit you again someday."

"You're always welcome."

As the older man headed back to the truck, Ezra turned to her. "You good? Ready to do this?"

She nodded, her jaw set. "Lead the way."

With a cluck of his tongue and gentle pressure with his knees, he set the horse in motion. Oreo followed Winny without hesitation. Three miles to McAlester Creek Trail, then another five to the high camp near the pass where they'd stay the night. Tomorrow the distance would be longer—ten miles—but mostly downhill until they dropped into Stehekin valley. The airstrip was located where the trail came out onto the flats north of Lake Chelan.

He'd get Haley there by her 4:00 p.m. rendezvous. Then she'd climb into her friend's plane and fly back to her life, in the same city where he lived half the year, but it might as well have been a different solar system for how separate their lives seemed.

And he would ride back with the two horses alone.

Alone. Funny how depressing that word sounded.

TWELVE

Haley's entire body hurt by the time they reached the horse camp. The trail had remained fairly level, traveling through forest along a creek much of the way, but over the last two miles, the horses had climbed over two thousand feet to reach a lake. They'd go even higher tomorrow, up and over a pass before descending on the far side.

She had to admit, though, despite her aching bones, she could see the allure of being out here. Had she ever gone this long without hearing a car honk? Not since adulthood, at least. No sounds of traffic, no huge truck engines, no delivery vehicles beeping as they backed up. No alarm clock, no uncomfortable high heels, no spending half an hour applying a mask of makeup to fit into a managerial position she wasn't sure she truly wanted.

No mask at all, not with those men after her. And not with Ezra. He'd seen through it from the very beginning anyway. Even more amazing, he seemed to like her for who she was, not who she projected herself to be. And certainly not for what he could get out of the relationship. All he'd gotten so far was his life put in danger.

She waited as he slipped off his horse and tied the

reins to a hitch rail at the campsite. Not only did the site have the requisite backcountry toilet, but there was also a built-in firepit surrounded by log benches.

Ezra came over to her, ready to help if she needed it. She'd managed a decent dismount earlier in the day when they stopped for lunch, but that was back when she could still feel her legs.

She unhooked her right foot from the stirrup and swung her leg around, feeling blindly for the ground. Once her boot connected, she pulled the other foot free. Easy. Until that second leg wobbled, protesting the way she'd treated it all day.

Before she fell, Ezra's strong hands wrapped around her waist. Her breath hitched at the sudden warmth and the fact they now stood facing each other, only inches apart. Tension crackled between them as Haley forced her gaze away from his lips and up to his eyes.

"Steady now?" His voice was husky.

"I'm good." She cleared her throat, forcing her feet to move a step backward. His hands fell back to his sides.

No kissing. That would definitely *not* help the situation. But oh, how she wanted to.

Together they unpacked the gear, tended the horses and set up camp. They'd both spent the day checking over their shoulders, but there'd been no sign of the armed men. Was it too much to hope they'd lost the trail and given up?

Unlike the last time they'd camped, this time Haley and Ezra each had their own small tent with sleeping bag. Rob and Nina had sent along a portable cookstove with freeze-dried trail meals, similar to what she'd eaten with Ezra, but Nina had made these herself. The difference was easy to see and smell as Haley stirred water into hers next to their small campfire.

She took a deep breath, her mouth watering at the scent of chicken and broccoli. "Pasta primavera, what a treat."

Ezra took a seat beside her on one of the logs circling the firepit. "See? Trail food can be delicious."

"Honestly, I think it's all this time in the open air. Everything out here just tastes better."

His eyes twinkled. "Maybe we'll turn you into a hiker yet."

"It *is* really beautiful, away from the city. I can see why you love it so much." She glanced at him shyly, then just as quickly looked back at her food as heat built in her cheeks. Somehow the comment felt too personal, like she was revealing how much she'd been paying attention. Which was silly because anybody could see Ezra and the outdoors were made for each other.

As they ate, the evening light slowly faded into the muted purples and pinks of sunset. Stars were twinkling overhead by the time they'd cleaned up the meal and settled the horses for the night. The fire had burned down to hot, glowing embers when Haley pulled herself to her feet.

"I'm beat." She stretched in a vain attempt to loosen her sore muscles.

"Get some sleep. I'll stay up out here a little longer."

The forest around them had grown so dark, she could no longer see the trail. "Do you think we'll be safe?"

He crossed one long leg over the other. "I think… I'll be glad when we get to the rendezvous tomorrow. But you don't need to worry."

She crossed her arms over her stomach, suddenly

chilled in the cool evening air. He'd chosen those words very carefully. "What do you think happened to them?" No need to specify *whom* she meant.

"Best case, once we drove off, they couldn't track us. Worst case..." His voice went quiet, and she could imagine all the scenarios running through his mind.

Please keep the Callahans safe, she prayed silently.

"Worst case," he went on, "they *did* track us and have been biding their time to make a move. Somewhere in the middle is the possibility that when they don't find us on any of the roads, they guess we're heading into Stehekin and catch up with us at some point."

She shivered.

"Haley, don't worry about it. You need sleep." He rose to his feet and before she quite knew what was happening, he had enfolded her in his strong arms. "I'm going to protect you, no matter what."

For a long moment, she disappeared into his warmth, letting go of the terrors of the last few days and the bleak road ahead. She'd forgotten what it felt like to let someone else help and comfort her, to not *always* have to be strong. How long had it been? Since she was a girl and her mother used to hold her close?

When he stepped back, the cold returned to bite at her bones and she ducked into her tent without lingering so he wouldn't see the sheen of tears gathering in her eyes yet again.

Not until she was curled up in her sleeping bag did she let the tears out.

Ezra sat back down on the log and flung tiny twigs into the dying fire, watching them flare up if they landed close enough to the hot coals. It was getting harder and harder to deny his feelings for Haley. As much as he wanted to pretend he was only concerned and protective because that was his job as a law enforcement officer, he knew it wasn't true. Haley stirred up something much deeper inside him than any woman had since Sarah.

And it was utterly terrifying.

Hadn't he gone through enough heartbreak already? Falling for Haley would only set him up for more of the same. She had so many things going on right now, there was no way she could even consider a relationship. And by her own admission, she didn't trust anyone's intentions after that louse made a show of her at that ball game. She would've been miserable with a man like that, using her to gain his own celebrity status... The twig in Ezra's hand snapped and he forced his fingers to relax.

Sure, she seemed to enjoy his company. She *had* melted into his arms. But with all the trauma she'd endured in the last few days, maybe that was a perfectly natural reaction.

He couldn't settle for anything less than he'd had with Sarah...and he wasn't sure he could risk his heart again like that. Even if Haley told him she had feelings for him, there were too many things that could go wrong, too many ways to sink back under the dark, endless clouds of loss and despair.

Flicking another small chunk into the fire, he listened as she rustled inside her tent. Tomorrow, less than twenty-four hours from now, they'd part ways. All the more reason not to indulge his unruly emotions. Minutes passed and she grew quiet within the tent. His own sleeping bag sounded awfully appealing, but he couldn't risk it. Not with the possibility of those men still on the loose. Setting up his tent had been more for Haley's benefit than anything else.

If anyone snuck up on them in the dark, they needed every possible second of advance warning. He shook his head, trying to clear away the sleepiness pressing close, and stretched.

The horses were hitched close by, rustling softly as they nosed about in the grass, but otherwise the night was quiet. Overhead, the full glory of a Cascadian night sky was on display, millions of stars twinkling against the backdrop of the Milky Way, painted like a giant white strip against the blackness.

A soft whicker broke the stillness, then what sounded like pawing at the ground. A snort. *Almost* like the horses were nervous. Probably some nocturnal animal drifting close while hunting. He'd made sure to secure all their gear and the horse feed up in a tree. Wild animals usually steered clear of pack horses because of the scent of human all over the area, but every now and then one got hungry enough to venture close.

Best to check on them. He rose from the log where he'd been sitting, his hand drifting to his utility belt with the flashlight and handgun, but he didn't draw, either. His eyes had adjusted enough to make out the dark shapes of the tents and trees in the distance. He headed in the direction of the noise, careful of each step in the darkness, though the site was smooth and grassy.

The hitching rail became visible—a stripe of black against a dark backdrop. But where were the horses?

His chest tightened. It was dark—maybe they'd worked themselves loose and he couldn't see them. He pulled out the flashlight but held off flipping it on as he worked his way around the hitching rail. No reason to broadcast his location until absolutely necessary.

The hairs stood up on the back of his neck as he strained to see in the darkness, almost like he could *feel* something out of place. His finger played over the ridged surface of the flashlight button, but he resisted the urge to press it. Maybe he'd better wake Haley before he ventured any farther from camp. Just to be safe.

He sensed the motion behind him before he saw the dark blur from the corner of his eye. Something hard pressed into his back below his left shoulder blade. His heart sank even as adrenaline flooded his system.

"Halt," a man's voice commanded in a low, rough whisper. "Hands on your head and don't make a sound." Foreign accent, but not Russian this time. Maybe German?

Trying to figure it out gave him something to think about besides how he'd broken his promise to keep Haley safe.

He lifted his hands slowly, still gripping the flashlight. The man promptly patted his sides until he found Ezra's gun and the knife in his belt. Which meant that wasn't an AK-47 at his back—no way could the man keep it in place with one hand and still manage to search him, unless his arms were long as a gorilla's. Not that that fact helped him much. A gun was still a gun.

If he called out to warn Haley, how fast would the man shoot? Probably not the best choice. Even clicking on the flashlight might clue her in, if the light were enough to wake her, but was it too risky?

Before he could decide, more voices came from the direction of the tents, filling his insides with dread.

"She's here. Got the camera too." This time it *was* the

Russian they'd tied up, which meant nobody from the park service had managed to stumble over him before his comrades found him. A lantern kicked on, casting long shadows across the ground.

"Where are my horses?" he demanded, infusing his voice with strength. "I'm a ranger with the National Park Service, and I'm placing you under arrest."

The man laughed. "Your horses are ours now, and you're in no position to arrest anyone." He ushered Ezra back toward the tents and pushed him down on one of the logs next to Haley, who was pale-faced and blinking in the harsh light of the lantern. Her blond hair was mussy on one side from her sleeping bag, and she had the wide-eyed look of someone who'd just been yanked out of a deep sleep. Worst of all was the way her hands trembled on top of her head.

"You okay?" he asked, keeping his voice low.

A sudden blow to the back of his head made him wince in pain. "No talking. I'll take that." A different man snatched the flashlight out of Ezra's grasp. He stalked around to stand in front of them on the other side of the firepit. The blond Russian handed the guy Haley's camera, suggesting this man must be their leader. Haley stiffened, and Ezra longed to reach over and take her hand, but he didn't dare move.

The leader fiddled with the camera, his movements hard to see in the lantern light, but it was obvious when he triumphantly held up the SD card. "Got it. Tie them," he ordered, "while I call the boss."

Tie them was better than *shoot them*, but how long would this reprieve last? Why would they need either Haley or Ezra alive now? As the man stalked off, one of the others tugged Ezra's hands off his head and tied them behind his back with a plastic zip tie that bit into his skin. Haley grimaced as she received the same treatment.

The man who'd taken the SD card vanished out of reach of the lantern light, far enough that his conversation was indistinguishable. He wasn't using a radio—there was no crackle of static, no return voice. Must be a satellite phone.

When he came back, Ezra exchanged a glance with Haley. Her throat bobbed but she lifted her chin. He loved that about her, that courage and defiance despite the danger.

"Boss says keep them alive until he can ask them questions," the leader announced.

Good. That meant they had a little more time to cobble together a way out of this mess.

"Chris Collins?" Haley practically spat the words. "Is that your boss?"

The nearest man slapped her across the mouth. "Shut up!"

Anger sparked hot beneath Ezra's ribs but he kept his backside firmly attached to the log, despite the nearly overpowering desire to ram the man in the stomach. Getting himself killed, or even incapacitated, wouldn't help Haley.

"Hansen, Petrov," the leader said, "you two are on guard." He nodded toward the tents. "Belsky and I are getting some shut-eye."

They stalked off, leaving the one with the German accent, presumably Hansen, and a brown-haired man Ezra didn't recognize. Four in total, which meant either they'd failed to find the other one he'd tied up back in the glacial valley, or he'd stayed with whoever was driving that SUV. Hopefully he'd been found by rangers and arrested.

Behind him, the tent zippers opened and closed. Their remaining guards waited silently for a moment, then one of them muttered something under his breath and kicked the ground savagely. Apparently the man wasn't happy with their assignment. Good—that could be helpful for him and Haley.

They walked around the firepit and seated themselves on the ground, their backs against the log on the opposite side, maybe ten feet away.

"Don't budge," Hansen ordered, keeping his gun firmly pointed at Ezra.

The other one, Petrov, didn't seem terribly worried about a possible escape attempt, because he laid his gun aside long enough to dig a flask out of his coat pocket and take a long swig before passing it to Hansen. Ezra used their momentary distraction to inch slowly closer to Haley, until with a little careful maneuvering they could touch each other's fingers. It wasn't much of a way to communicate, but it was *something*.

By his reckoning it was still early, nearing midnight, which gave them plenty of long hours to wait for an opportunity. After squeezing Haley's fingers, Ezra yawned, letting his chin droop toward his chest. Given the past few days, feigning exhaustion wasn't difficult.

After a couple of minutes, Haley did likewise, rolling her head as if she were fighting off fatigue. Across from them, the AK-47 still lay on the ground and Hansen draped his gun arm across one bent knee. The men talked quietly to each other, casting glances less and less frequently at the captives.

Not actually falling asleep was a challenge, as was

not toppling off the log, but Ezra managed to stay upright and periodically crack open an eye to check the guards. As silently as he could, he twisted his arms to one side and wriggled his fingers into a pocket on his utility belt, pulling out a length of paracord. Neither of the guards looked up from the card game they'd started, and they'd taken the lantern to their side of the firepit, leaving him and Haley on the periphery of the light.

The zip tie was tight, but he managed to work one end of the cord up through a small gap on one side of his overlapping wrists. The other two ends he looped through his belt and tied off in a secure knot. Haley glanced his direction more than once, as if she were dying to know what he was doing, but he made sure to keep up the act of dozing. Now it was only a matter of gently sawing the tie back and forth on the paracord, until friction made the plastic give way enough for him to snap his wrists apart.

He tested out the system slowly at first, afraid the rhythmic sound might attract the guards' attention, but their chatter was enough to cover the noise. Time crawled past and the stars shifted overhead, familiar constellations giving way to other old friends as the earth rotated. The moon would rise soon. How long had it been? Would these two ever fall asleep, or would the others wake up to replace them?

Just when he thought they might need a new plan, he glanced across the firepit to see both guards with their heads tipped back against the log. He'd been working at the plastic tie for a solid half hour, maybe longer, but he didn't want to risk doing the actual breaking until he and Haley left the camp—just in case the sound was loud.

He nudged Haley, whose eyes popped open as she jerked upright. The lantern was still going strong, but it had tipped over sometime in the last hour and now sent most of its glow toward the ground and the two sleeping guards. Perfect.

His muscles and joints creaked in protest as he slowly shifted his weight forward and stood. For a second, he paused, wondering if even that telltale bit of human motion in the silent forest would be enough to give them away. But no one stirred.

Haley stood too, then followed as he picked his way through the lighted area near the firepit. Once they reached the edge of the light's glow, there'd be virtually no way to see what was on the ground. No way to make sure they didn't step on crackling sticks and dead leaves. But thankfully the grassy campsite didn't hide any obstacles, and a few minutes later he had found the trail itself.

The going was tricky, with their hands still behind their backs, but he didn't want to risk the noise of snapping the ties. Not yet. He had to feel his way forward for each step, testing the ground before shifting his weight, ignoring the urge to run and get Haley as far away from those men as he could.

But no sounds came from the campsite behind them, and after half an hour of tentative scrambling up the ever-steepening path, he paused to twist his wrists apart. The torque was enough to break the plastic tie and he rubbed his chafed skin as Haley stared at him.

"How'd you do that?" she whispered.

"I'll show you." He untied the paracord from his belt and looped it through her tie, then worked it back and forth rapidly. Without the potential audience, it took a fraction of the time. "Now twist your wrists apart. It might hurt a bit."

She complied, then rubbed her wrists too. "Oh, that feels so much better."

He stooped to retrieve the plastic pieces off the ground and stuffed them into his pocket. No reason to litter. He *was* still a park ranger—for the moment, at least. Who knew what the chief ranger would do with him after this little escapade was over?

That was a problem for another day. What mattered now was getting Haley up and over the mountain pass and down into Stehekin. They'd lost their horses, their supplies and the SD card, but he still had the backup flash drive stashed inside his pocket. If those men kept sleeping a little longer, they'd have enough of a head start to make it.

He set his jaw as he turned back up the steep, rocky path. They *had* to make it.

THIRTEEN

Haley passed the long night in a haze of exhaustion, too tired to feel afraid as she stumbled along the rocky trail after Ezra. Her legs burned from the exertion, and she had a moment at the top of the pass where the wind hit her full in the face, and she knew if she could see anything that the view would be spectacular, but there was nothing but endless darkness and aching feet and stubbed toes and walking. Always walking.

The thing that kept her going was knowing that soon this nightmare would be over. God had provided Ezra's help, and through him, a backup copy of that video file, and within hours she'd be safely in Ford's plane. She could still untangle this mess and get back to life the way it was meant to be.

Something uncomfortable wriggled deep inside, but she doggedly shoved the feeling aside. Her father had picked her as the next CEO, God had blessed her efforts and it was time to claim that position and see that Chris got the justice he deserved. Someday she'd have time to do research again. Just because she'd caught a glimpse out here of another way didn't mean she needed to change her plans. She'd experienced that beautiful moment of God's grace and felt His presence so strongly the other morning. There was no reason she couldn't keep dwelling in close relationship with Him now that she was heading back.

She already attended weekly church, but maybe she could volunteer more. Or squeeze in another Bible study. God could fit into her life. *Right, Lord?*

The unsettled feeling grew, almost like a bad taste in her mouth she couldn't get rid of. In front of her, Ezra's lean frame was only visible as a darker mass against the dark mountain trail. Despite the heartbreak he'd endured, he was so easygoing, so relaxed, like stress wasn't part of his life until she showed up. He had such an open, warm heart, and an enduring faith that anchored him through the storms of life. Unlike her, he wasn't rushing to and fro trying to be everything to everyone else.

Well, clearly that meant they were on different paths. God had called him to the right life for him, and He'd called Haley to the corporate world in the city. This underlying sense of disappointment and yearning was perfectly natural after everything they'd experienced together. She'd get over it, just like she'd gotten over that deep-seated dream of working in R&D doing science, and that momentary vision of a life shared with someone else before she'd realized the truth about Xander.

She swallowed the nagging sense of disappointment and kept plodding onward, one step after another. Hours passed, each like the one before it, as she stared at Ezra's back in the dark. Once or twice he asked if she wanted a break, but she said no. If she stopped now, her legs might refuse to get going again.

At least they hadn't heard any sign of their pursuers,

but only the soft thumping of their boots on the path until the first early birdcalls broke the silence. By now they were traipsing downhill on the long, winding descent into Stehekin Valley. Far in the distance, a narrow lake gleamed in the faint predawn light like a strip of black satin ribbon.

The sun crept up over the mountain peaks in the east, casting a golden-pink glow across the woods around them and valley below. The lake changed from a gloomy black swamp to a glittering golden jewel surrounded by rich green forest. Haley breathed deeply, inhaling the fertile scent of earth and ancient trees and the dry dustiness of the rocks. Nothing like the air she was used to. It was strange, really, how despite the terror of the last few days, she felt at peace out here. They were fleeing for their lives, and yet the world around them moved at the same slow, steady pace, never hurried.

As the sun rose and they descended, Ezra paused to point to the land below. A stream ran down from the mountains, across a plain, and emptied into the lake, like a line someone had drawn with a pen across the landscape. "That's Lake Chelan. The village of Stehekin is just around the east side. Your airstrip is north on that plain, on the far side of Stehekin River."

She squinted in the sunlight, looking for any shiny, silver objects that might indicate an airplane down there. With the forested ridges converging on both sides of the plain, it would be a difficult approach. "Looks challenging."

"Not many people use it, to be honest. Float planes are a lot more popular." His face was worn, with dark circles under his eyes, and the usual twinkle had been replaced by something dull. Like he'd also been lost in unpleasant thoughts.

She'd put him in a lot of danger. And his job would be in jeopardy too. Words of gratitude seemed hopelessly inadequate, but she had to try. As he started walking again, she called softly after him, "Ezra, I know I've said it a million times and it can't begin to repay what you've done for me but, thank you."

He glanced back, smiling, but the haunted look still lingered. "You're welcome. God put me in the right place at the right time."

She swallowed, trying to dig up the courage to ask what was bothering him. "Is your job going to be okay here? Since you didn't turn me in? I hate to think I could've cost you something you love so much."

"Don't worry about it. It'll be all right." He said it while he walked, his gaze on the trail ahead, and while his voice carried his usual conviction, guilt still ate at her insides.

Something was bothering him. But then, she could hardly expect him to go through an experience like this and not be affected. She couldn't help thinking these days had somehow become pivotal in her life, and even though she was going to fix everything, she couldn't completely go back to being the same person she'd been before.

By late morning, they reached the last of the hiker camps and turned off the main trail they'd been following to make the final descent into the valley. Haley's back was covered with sweat from the heat that had risen with the sun, and she felt like she hadn't slept or eaten in a week. After a final round of switchbacks— she'd be fine if she never saw a switchback again—the trail took them out onto the plain, where arms of the river flowed amid wildflowers and tall grasses swaying in the morning breeze. An actual road—gravel, but still, a road—stretched in both directions down the center of the valley, running around the east side of the lake.

"I thought you couldn't drive into Stehekin?" she asked, pointing at it.

A smile brought a glimpse of a twinkle to his eyes. "You can't. But you can catch a bus in Stehekin to bring you up to the airstrip, or to the ranches a little farther in."

"How did they get a bus in here?"

"*That* is an excellent question. We've got a few hours until your friend arrives. Want to see the town? We can get something to eat."

Doing something normal? With Ezra? A little thrill danced through her system. But… "Won't you get in trouble? I mean if anybody recognizes you?"

He shrugged. "I'm not in uniform. And I rarely come out this far. As long as we act like tourists, it'll be okay. Plus—" he glanced over his shoulder, toward the mountain trail "—if they're still after us, they'll be less likely to search in town."

Despite everything, a smile curled her lips. "I'm in. Let's do it."

They didn't have to walk far down the road before a bus came rolling up behind them, kicking up a plume of dust in its wake. Ezra flagged the driver, who pulled to a stop. After paying their fares, he led the way to a pair of empty seats.

"Thanks." She slipped into the seat next to the window, a moan escaping her lips at the delicious sensation of sitting down. "I'm glad you had some cash."

"I always keep some stashed away in my belt. Just for emergencies."

"Does this sort of thing happen to you often?"

"Thankfully, this is a first. You've brought a whole new level of chaos to my life." His lips quirked.

Gorgeous mountain scenery rolled past outside the windows like they were driving through a postcard. A ranch sprawled out on the left side of the bus—a big house with a wide front porch like the Callahans', surrounded by split rail fences and green fields of grazing horses. She leaned her shoulder against Ezra, settling into his warmth, and sighed contentedly.

As the bus skirted the northern end of the lake, the plains gave way to forest again. Small buildings appeared intermittently between the trees on one side, and docks and boats dotted the edge of the lake on the other.

"Do people live up here year-round?" she asked.

"Yeah, about eighty of them. There's even a one-room schoolhouse for kindergarten through eighth grade."

"And once you hit high school?"

He shrugged. "Homeschool? Or you can hop on the ferry down to Chelan, but it's an hour each direction."

They disembarked in front of what looked like the world's tiniest post office, then whiled away the next hour browsing the gift shop, buying pastries and sitting on the end of a dock with their feet dangling in the water.

What would life be like, to feel this content all the time? Haley took a bite of her cherry Danish and glanced at Ezra. "Can I ask you something?"

"Anything. You practically know my life story by now."

A definite exaggeration, but she smiled shyly all the same. "Is this what it's usually like out here for you?"

His brows pulled together. "Eating pastries next to a lake with a beautiful woman? You don't have a very high opinion of park rangers, do you?"

"That wasn't what I meant. If you're representative of all rangers, I think they're amazing. Brave. Heroic." Heat crept into her cheeks, but it wasn't from the words that had popped out unchecked. No, her mind had snagged on something he'd said. *Beautiful*. She'd been complimented plenty of times, but it never meant as much to her as it did right now, coming from him. "I meant, this sense of peace. Like the whole world could be crumbling out there—" she gestured to the mountains "—and it wouldn't matter, because right here, right now, there's peace. Wholeness."

He plucked a crumb off his shirt and flicked it into the lake, staring across the water for a moment. When he looked back at her, something had shifted in his gaze, his dark eyes taking on an intensity that stole the air from her lungs. "Can I be honest?"

"Yeah." The word came out as a mere breath.

"I haven't felt like that in a long time. Not since…" His dead wife's name hovered between them, unspoken. But instead of clouding over with sorrow, his eyes stayed clear, like he wasn't looking at the past anymore but rather toward the future. "But when I'm with you, Haley, I feel alive. Whole. I—" He broke off, staring down at his hands for a moment, then rubbed the back of his neck. "Sorry, words aren't helping me out right now."

Her heart thudded inside her chest as she rested a hand on his arm. What exactly was he saying? What did she *want* him to say? He'd opened up to her—that fact alone made joy surge through her insides. "No, I get it.

I get what you mean. I haven't gone through the same things you have, but I've spent my life searching for *something*. Trying to find the place where I fit in, where I'm doing what I'm supposed to be doing, and now..."

Her voice trailed away as her brain caught up to her mouth. What on earth was *she* saying? That she finally felt at home, in this gorgeous place? But it wasn't really about the place, was it?

She cut off the thought before it could go any farther. There was no reason to indulge in this line of thinking, not when everything was already a horrible mess. *Put out one fire at a time, Haley. Don't start a new one. Remember Xander?* Maybe everything with Ezra would change once they weren't in this high-stress situation.

His voice, low and rough, cut into her disorderly thoughts. "I hope you can find the right path, Haley. The one that brings you peace."

As if to punctuate his words, the high whirring of an airplane engine echoed across the valley. A dark speck moved against the bright backdrop of blue ever closer from the south.

Ezra glanced at his wristwatch then nodded toward it. "We'd better get moving. That's probably your friend."

Words hovered on her tongue, heavy and unspoken, but the approaching aircraft seemed to steal them away. Truth was, she had nothing to say. Not even, *I hope you find the right path too*, because the moment was lost, and Ezra was standing up and holding out his hand for her without meeting her eyes.

She slipped her socks and boots back on, tied up the laces and let him lead the way toward the airplane that would take her out of his life forever.

* * *

Ezra kept his gaze anywhere but on Haley as they climbed off the bus near the dirt road leading to the Stehekin airstrip. She'd already confirmed what he'd suspected—the small, low-winged Cirrus plane belonged to Ford Anderson.

Of course, given the other thing she'd confirmed—that she was ready to move on with her life, apart from him—this fact shouldn't have created such a dogged sense of disappointment. Maybe sharing his emotions so openly had been a bad idea, especially given his own uncertainties about even the possibility of a relationship, but it hadn't seemed honest to keep it all to himself. No, he'd at least needed to see what she was thinking and feeling, and she'd made it abundantly clear.

Everything she'd said had been about her career and finding the right fit, nothing about him or how she felt with him. He hadn't even known her a week, and he could tell her a thing or two about herself—like to turn over that position as CEO to someone else. Let them have all the stress while she could live her dream of doing research. Yet she stubbornly clung onto what she thought everyone else wanted from her.

There wasn't any point getting riled up about what decisions Haley made though, because she was about to walk out of his life for good. A tiny part of him silently rejoiced. His love for Sarah and Kaitlyn—the family they'd created, the memories they'd shared—those were safe forever. No new woman could steal them away. But that tiny part wasn't enough to remove this heavy feeling of dread weighing down each step as they walked toward the taxiing plane.

They waited in silence near the edge of the airstrip until the plane stopped moving. The engine still hummed loudly as one of the doors popped open over a wing and an older man climbed out. Between his gray business suit and meticulously styled salt-and-pepper hair, he looked like one of those store-window models for the Men's Wearhouse. Another one of the beautiful people of the world, like Haley, who moved in the top circles of society and had enough money to buy his own private plane.

Ezra dug into the ground with the toe of his boot. No wonder Haley didn't need *him*. He cleared his throat and glanced between her and the man. "Is that him? Your father's lawyer?"

She nodded, a sheen of moisture glistening in her eyes. So happy to be free of her experience here.

"Haley!" the man called over the noise of the engine as he walked up to them. He pressed a kiss to each of her cheeks, then stood back, examining her with both hands on her shoulders. "You all right, my dear?"

"Yes." She blinked, swiping covertly at her cheeks. "Thanks to Ezra. He's a park ranger here. Ezra, this is Ford Anderson."

Ford extended a hand and shook Ezra's firmly. "Thank you for looking after her. I'll make sure she's taken care of." He seemed like a capable, confident man, but the words felt like a dismissal. *You've done your part, now get back to work.* He turned to Haley. "Ready to go?"

"Just give me a minute…to say goodbye." Her throat bobbed, and the words came out thick, like all the emotion she'd kept pent up during their ordeal was finally about to break loose now that she was with Ford. His heart twisted despite himself—he'd done everything he could to keep her safe, and now he had to turn her over to someone else and watch her walk away.

The older man glanced between the two of them and nodded toward the plane. "I'll be waiting."

"Ezra..." Haley paused, like she was searching for the right words. But nothing made *goodbye* any easier, did it? Besides acting like you were fine?

"Here." He fished the backup flash drive out of his pocket and pressed it into her hand. "Don't forget this. God go with you, Haley. I hope you find what you're looking for."

She nodded, blinking again. "Thank you. For everything. I... I'll..." Her head dropped and she stared at her feet for a moment.

From the plane, Ford called, "We'd better get moving. No time to lose."

For a second, some wild part of him wanted to take her in his arms, sweep her off her feet and kiss her breathless. Then tell her he never wanted to be away from her again. But how could he follow that impulse when their lives were so different? And that part of him that would always tie him to Sarah and Kaitlyn... how could he offer something he couldn't truly give?

He stuffed his hands deep into his pockets. "Goodbye, Haley."

"Goodbye, Ezra." Her throat bobbed again, and she backed up a few steps closer to the plane. She turned away, but just as he thought she would head for the plane, she pivoted to face him once more.

She crossed the distance between them, stopping just in front of him and stealing the air from his lungs. They stood frozen for the span of a heartbeat until she leaned forward, pressing a soft, lingering kiss to his cheek. Her face was stricken as she pulled back. He reached for her, more out of impulse than any conscious thought, but she'd already turned away to the plane.

This time she didn't look back.

FOURTEEN

Haley choked back the sob threatening to burst out and forced her attention onto the mountains and forest ahead. Anywhere but looking down at the green jewel of a valley, where a man stood holding a piece of her heart.

"Are you all right, Haley?" Ford asked, his voice filled with concern. "You've been missing for days. Did you get hurt?"

Only her heart, but she wasn't about to tell him that. Instead, she drew in a deep, shuddering breath. "No, nothing beyond some blisters, bruises and sore muscles, thankfully."

He glanced away from the front window to eye her critically. "What about the camera?"

"I lost it. Chris's men caught up with us last night. But I've got this backup we made." She held out the flash drive. He took it and slipped it into his suit jacket.

"Good. I've already arranged a meeting with your father and an FBI agent at the office, since you're concerned about the police. We'll untangle this mess. Do you have any idea who he's working with?"

"I think it's the same Swiss company who offered the deal on the new engine prototype last year, the one that my father thought was a front for the Russian government. Those men after us were well-trained and well-armed, plus at least two of them were Russian. They kept referring to their boss. It's got to be Chris."

Ford sucked on his lower lip. "Sounds plausible. He was angry about getting passed over as CEO, so he opted for revenge and money instead."

"Exactly."

She settled back into the seat, letting her mind churn over the problem at hand and the facts of the case. Anything other than Ezra Dalton.

Everything was going to work out fine now. She'd accomplished what she wanted. She was safe in Ford's plane, with assurance of his help, and soon her father and the authorities would understand how Chris had deceived them. *Thanks, Lord.*

But as the Seattle skyline, with its tall, glass-covered buildings and distinctive Space Needle, came into view, uneasiness nudged her stomach. Yes, she was going back, but she wasn't entirely sure she wanted to. This whole time she'd been looking to escape the wilderness, and she hadn't realized how the wilderness had actually *been* an escape. Now she had to face it all again—the hectic, stress-filled days, the demanding schedule, the nights without sleep. Her empty apartment. The lack of time for God or deep human connection.

That pastry she'd eaten sat like a rock inside her stomach.

The flight was short, and before she was ready, Ford had eased the plane down onto the same runway she'd departed from only a few days before. Her heart twinged as she glanced at the family hangar. She'd never pull into it again in her same little Cessna. She'd left its wreckage behind along with that piece of her heart in the North Cascades.

A black car was waiting outside the hangar. Anxiety prickled like sharp nails as she watched to see if anyone would unroll the windows and start shooting, but no one did. *Thank You, Lord.* Hopefully her pursuers had no idea she'd returned to Seattle.

And as illogical as it was, just being with Ford made her feel like everything was going to be okay. He'd always been a role model to her, like her father—a man who moved confidently through life, doing and getting exactly what he wanted, perfectly at ease no matter the situation. Not bluffing his way through, the way she was.

She slipped inside the empty hangar to wash her face in the restroom. Her business suit was still folded up in one of the lockers—she could change her clothes and at least pretend to have things under control. But what was the point now? Besides, this Cascades T-shirt was all she had left of Ezra. A soft, woodsy scent of cedar still clung to it.

She swallowed the lump in her throat as she climbed into the back seat of the car next to Ford. Her sense of dread grew with each mile as they approached her father's office. Probably because she would have to face her father, explain everything, answer all their questions, on top of already feeling beat-up and exhausted. But she'd get used to being back here. She would.

Rather than pulling up a side street to the front entrance, the driver turned into the garage. Haley raised an eyebrow at Ford as the dim, orange glow of artificial lighting replaced late-afternoon sunshine.

"We wanted to avoid the press, along with what's left

of the office crowd," he said, "so we'll take the elevator directly from the lower level rather than go through the lobby."

Probably wise, although it had to be well after 6:00 p.m. by now. That meant they'd be avoiding security too, as they could use a key card to enter the building and access the elevator.

The car descended to the lowest level of the garage, pulling to a stop in front of the access door to sublevel B. Haley only entered this way when she came in at odd hours—she preferred to enter through the lobby, which felt far more professional and less clandestine than a dingy white metal door leading into a cinder-block sublevel.

Ford held the car door for her as she climbed out. She waited as he swiped his card, then followed him inside toward the elevator. The building had several, all accessed from the lobby, but only one descended this far.

As they approached, the door dinged open on its own. A lone man stepped out, impeccably dressed in a navy blue suit and red tie, but his build was all wrong to be her father.

Her muscles froze. It was Chris Collins.

Ezra wasn't sure how much time had passed since Haley's plane had vanished into the bright blue expanse of the sky. He'd stood watching for a long time after she climbed into the cockpit. As the plane whirred past him, building up speed and lifting into the air. As it changed from a giant locust to a bumblebee to a tiny gnat, then vanished.

Even then he had stared, as if in a dream, at the fluffy white clouds drifting past like cotton balls. Until finally he'd faced the truth—she was gone now, heading back to her life. It was time to head back to his.

He turned away from the airstrip and wandered back toward the dirt road, opting to walk back to Stehekin rather than catch a ride on the bus. Rob would be waiting for him, with the horse trailer, at the trailhead tomorrow evening. But with no supplies and those men on the trail, it made more sense to head to the ranger station and call for a chopper ride out than hike back. He'd have to explain everything anyway, and the sooner he did, the sooner they could start searching for Rob's horses.

Every step felt like lifting a rock rather than one of his own feet. The dirt road was empty by the time he reached it, and he tried to force himself to pick up the pace, mentally rehearsing the explanation he'd give his boss as he walked. His heart nearly leaped out of his chest when he heard a plane engine, but it was only a float plane. Not Haley.

By the time he reached the end of the lake, where the trees crowded the right side of the road, the sun was already slipping behind the mountains to the west. Surely Haley must be back in Seattle by now. At least it looked like Ford was taking her that direction. She'd never told him her plans beyond the rendezvous, had she?

He stepped off the road and into the trees as the bus trundled past again on another one of its runs up the valley. After the dust had cleared, he trudged back out onto the road.

Suddenly a dark form in camo fatigues stepped from out of the bushes, stopping directly in front of him, gun aimed at his chest. It was the blond Russian, Belsky. His three comrades followed immediately after him, surrounding Ezra before he realized what was happening.

"Got you this time," Belsky said, sneering.

Ezra raised his hands. "You're too late, she's already gone. You may as well let me go and give up."

The leader of the group zip-tied his hands together again and gripped his upper arm. "I don't think so. See, you're in deep enough the boss wants to see you. Guess that makes you special, doesn't it?"

The brown-haired one, Petrov, took his arm and dragged him across the empty road toward the lake. The float plane he'd seen land earlier was tied up a short distance away.

He dug in his heels, pulling back against Petrov's grasp. His odds of survival weren't great, but they'd be reduced to nil if the men flew off with him. At least out here somebody might overhear and be able to help.

But the second he resisted, something blunt crashed into the back of his head. Stars flickered as Ezra's vision grew dark. His fading consciousness clung like a lichen on a rock to one last thought. *At least Haley is safe.*

Haley's stomach dropped to her knees at the sight of Chris. Her brain scrambled to make the computation.

How did he know they were coming...?

Ford?

Chris's lips curled into a sneer. "Surprised to see me? Poor, innocent Haley, so convinced everyone is as dedicated to your father and his vision as you are."

She backed up instinctively but bumped into Ford, who wrapped his hands around her shoulders. "Sorry, my girl, I really do feel bad things had to work out this way. Betrayal is so pedestrian, but you walked right into my hands."

Her heart climbed into her throat. *No.* "But...but..."

she stammered, "I trusted you. And my dad. After all these years, how could you...?" There had to be some mistake, yet here he was, clutching her shoulders and pushing her toward Chris.

"An unfortunate side effect of not having the same goals in mind." He smiled, snakelike, sending a shiver slithering up her spine.

Chris tipped his head toward the whitewashed, cinder-block hallway. "Let's get her into the room."

Her mind whirled as he and Ford each took an arm and dragged her away from the elevator. Two armed guards, very much like the party she'd just left behind in the Cascades, materialized out of nowhere to follow them.

Had Ford been faking friendship with her father this whole time? She'd looked up to him all these years, and here he was, betraying their family. Had all of it been a lie?

"I don't get it," she insisted, anything to buy time while she figured out what they wanted. "How could you do this to us? To Dad?"

"Oh, James is a good man. He's been my friend since college. But people change, Haley, and they don't always see eye to eye." Ford barked a short laugh. "I told him to get off his moral high horse and *take the deal*. The payment would've been enough to make Whitcombe Aerotech the forerunner of its competitors, the Fortune 500 company I could've been at right now if I hadn't invested so much of my career in him. But no. He refused, our stocks plunged, and with the company in a precarious position, he picks *you* as his replacement. Despite half the board supporting Chris."

She didn't bother checking the sarcasm. "Because Chris is *obviously* a quality leader."

The younger man's chest puffed out next to her. "I'm not afraid to make bold decisions, and I've got years more experience than you. Whitcombe Aerotech won't grow without that kind of leadership. Besides—" he shot her a cocky grin "—I'm a man."

Her mouth fell open. *Of all the nerve.* "That has nothing to do with it. Did you ever consider that maybe my father doesn't want his business to become a mega-corporation? He resisted selling stock when you first wanted him to years ago, but he did it to keep the board happy. Apparently he didn't realize you'd stoop this low. Do you think pinning me for your crimes will make him listen?"

"And you—" she rounded on Ford "—you chose to work for him. You could've left whenever you wanted. You acted like *his friend*." Disgust filled her veins until she couldn't force out any more words.

Ford shrugged, a complacent smile plastered on his face. "It is what it is, Haley. When you grow up, maybe you'll learn that we're not all content spending our lives trying to please James Whitcombe."

Ouch. The jab stung, more so because it was true. But what Ford was doing—blaming her father for his life choices—was wrong. Haley might not be living her dreams, either, but that was entirely her fault. She had to take responsibility for her own decisions.

They stopped in front of one of the heavy, white metal doors lining the hallway. Chris rapped on it a few times, and another armed guard pushed it open from within. A lone metal chair stood in the center of the concrete floor. The ceiling was covered with pipes and ductwork, and a large furnace sat in the corner. From the way one of its panels hung off, it wasn't used anymore.

Ford and Chris dragged her inside and forced her into the chair, tying her ankles to the legs and her hands behind her back. Hard metal dug into the tender skin on the insides of her arms, cold even through her leather jacket. Chris felt inside both jacket pockets, coming away with her cell phone when he stepped back. As if she'd be able to call for help with her wrists tied together.

"Why are you doing this?" she demanded. "Your men destroyed the camera and now you have my only backup. What do you still want with me?"

Ford paused in the doorway, running an elegantly tapered finger up the door frame. "A person has to be flexible in this business, Haley. I was hoping to stay out of the whole messy affair entirely, but as you know, our men in the Cascades couldn't quite finish the job. And then you brought in that unfortunate park ranger…"

"Ezra?" she whispered. Was he still in danger?

But Ford had already left the room, and Chris only stopped to admonish her. "Don't waste your breath calling for help. I wouldn't want you to get hurt." He jerked his head toward the armed guard, whose face could've been etched out of stone.

Then he was gone.

Ezra blinked awake, aware that he was lying on his side. His stomach lurched as the seat beneath him dropped and then bounced up again. Right—the float plane. They were flying him out to question him. But where?

The plane was small—only a four-seater—and he took up the full back seat. Judging by his partial view, he'd guess that was Belsky in the front passenger seat. Who was flying? The leader?

His guess was confirmed when the pilot reached for the radio. "This is Dimitry. Get Anderson on the phone."

Anderson... Haley had left with Ford Anderson. It was a common last name, could be coincidence, but panic flared along his nerves anyway.

The radio crackled and a new voice spoke, one Ezra recognized immediately. "Anderson here. Report." His sudden urge to puke had nothing to do with the turbulence.

Haley wasn't safe at all—Ford Anderson was working *with* her enemies.

"We've got him," Dimitry answered. "Bring him to the building?"

"Yes. The woman is already secure. Anderson out."

Hot on the heels of his initial shock came a burning wave of anger. That man had *betrayed* Haley. He'd led her to believe he was going to help, and he'd taken her right to the enemy. *God, please protect her.*

Where were they keeping her? It didn't sound like he'd turned her over to the police. Hopefully they'd take him to the same place, where he could see for himself that she was okay and figure out some plan to get her out of this mess.

First, though, he had to do something about this zip tie around his wrists without the men in front noticing. They had yet to look back and see he was awake. Theoretically he could break through it the same way he had before—sufficient use of friction should weaken one section enough to let him snap it apart. But his paracord was gone, along with his utility belt. They must've removed it after knocking him out.

Slowly, so as not to make much noise, he groped along the back of the seat for anything he could use. His fingertips paused on a piece of metal wedged in the crevice between the seat and the seatback. It was hook-shaped and rough on one end, like part of a seat belt latch system that had broken. *Perfect.*

The whirring of the plane engine helped cover the noise as he rubbed the plastic across the hook. He misjudged the distance and ripped the metal across his skin once or twice, but the pain was minimal compared to thinking about what Haley might be enduring. Her emotional pain alone had to be crushing after Ford's betrayal.

Finally the zip tie loosened enough he could tell it was close to breaking. He lay still, debating the best time to make a move. The plane was descending—his ears kept popping—and in case they were going to take him to the same place as Haley, he needed to play helpless until he figured out where she was.

The plane came in for a choppy landing on what seemed like a large body of water, given what little he could see from his angle on the back seat. Orange-and-pink-hued sky filled the window over his head as the plane headed toward the dock. When it stopped, he kept his eyes shut tight and his body limp, giving no indication he'd ever come to.

"Still out," Belsky grunted. A minute later, a salty sea breeze filled the cabin as the doors opened.

A rough pair of hands hauled Ezra out of the plane. His feet thudded across a wooden dock as they dragged him to another back seat. He cracked an eye open to see it was a car this time.

Out the back window, twilight settled over the road and trees gave way to buildings. His pulse quickened as he passed something familiar. They were entering Seattle.

The plane must've landed in Puget Sound. Had they taken Haley back to her father's office? Was that the building they meant, or somewhere else? Some hidden warehouse where the police would never think to look? And why? Why keep them alive when surely killing them was the final plan?

He had a feeling he'd find out. And soon.

Haley dozed, head dropping forward until her chin rubbed against the collar of her jacket. How much time had passed? And the big question always burning in her mind—how long till they killed her?

A ringing knock on the metal door jerked her to attention. Chris strode in, still wearing the red tie, but his jacket was gone and he'd rolled up his sleeves. Another man followed, carrying a second metal chair, which he plunked down in front of Haley's.

Chris propped a foot up on the chair, his shiny Italian leather shoe glinting in the dim light. "How's it going, Haley?"

She gritted her teeth. "How do you *think* it's going, Chris?"

"Manners," he said, tsk-tsking. "I'd expect better for the future CEO."

"Don't you mean *from* the future CEO?"

"I don't think so, sweetheart."

"Don't you dare call me that. You've gotten everything you want." She glanced down at the chair and the ropes tying her in place. "What am I doing here?"

He took his foot off the other chair and paced back and forth behind it. "As it turns out, your father is a little more stubborn than I'd anticipated."

So maybe Dad hadn't just believed the worst. Her heart swelled.

Chris went on, "Despite all the evidence I so carefully planted to frame you, James seems to suspect there might be more going on. I had hoped once we caught you and recovered that video footage, Ford wouldn't have any trouble talking him into choosing me as your replacement—since you'll be in jail and all—but James is insisting on waiting out the trial."

"Must be frustrating not to get your way immediately," Haley snapped.

"It is." He stopped, straightening his tie as he looked at her. "But not to worry, we have a new plan. Ford is upstairs with dear old James right now. He's got all the paperwork drawn up to sign the business over and give me your share of the stock so I'll be the majority owner. All we're waiting on is the pièce de résistance—your confession."

"Right, as if that'll ever happen."

"You see," he continued as if she hadn't interrupted, "once James hears the words from your own mouth, he'll have no choice but to admit we're right. That his sweet daughter isn't who she's been pretending to be."

Haley sat up straighter. She *had* been pretending—at least about her desire to lead the company—but her father's loyalty and faith in her weren't misplaced. "Not gonna happen."

"Well, actually—" his lips split in a devious smile

"—I think it might." He glanced at the door, where another guard appeared. "Ready?"

The man nodded and handed him a tablet. Her chest squeezed as Chris carried it over and propped it up on the chair across from her. On the screen was what looked like a live feed from another room like hers—white cinder-block walls lined with pipes and ductwork, a single metal chair in the center on the gray concrete floor.

A camo-clad guard blocked her view of everything but the chair's legs. She held her breath, waiting until he stepped aside. The world froze.

Strapped in the chair, head lolling to one side and dried blood crusted on his temple, was Ezra.

FIFTEEN

"Let him go," Haley ordered, though her voice snagged on the words. "He doesn't have anything do to with this."

"Actually," Chris said, "he does. Thanks to you, he could testify against us. Even without hard evidence, the word of an honest park ranger might carry weight with a jury."

"You can't just…*kill* him." But Chris could, couldn't he? After what he'd done to that security guard the night he'd tried to steal the plans, she had no doubt what he was capable of.

"So here's the thing, Haley." He gave her the same look she'd seen her father give clueless new employees as he patiently explained something. "If you confess, I won't need to make sure the ranger stays silent. Your admission of guilt will trump any protest he might try to make."

Her mouth fell open. She glanced from Chris to the tablet and back again. Why, of all the low, nasty—

"You're using him to get what you want out of me."

He scowled. "Don't bother sounding so disgusted. This is why you'd never have made the right leader.

Like your father, you're not willing to make the tough choices. *Fortes fortuna juvat.* Fortune aids the brave."

"Killing people, stealing and framing the innocent *isn't* brave," she spat.

He waved a hand as if to dismiss her words. "I'm not here to argue ethics. I'm here to let you know the situation. It's quite simple. We record your confession and share it live with your father and Ford upstairs. He signs the paperwork, my men take your ranger back to his wilderness and the police escort you to jail. If you're still feeling reluctant, we can provide more incentive." Without waiting for her response, he spoke into his phone. "Punch him."

A guard flashed into view on the tablet screen and smashed a fist into the side of Ezra's face. It hurt to watch. The rope tied around Ezra's chest kept him from flying out of the chair. His head bounced to one side and he groggily shook it, glaring up at the guard and spitting out a mouthful of blood.

"Again?" Chris looked at her.

"No! Stop hurting him!"

"Then I need your confession." His lips curled into a smile, but his eyes were ice cold.

God, how do we get out of this mess? There *had* to be a way. Surely His plan wasn't to let the bad guys win? If only she had time to think, maybe she could figure out a solution. She had to get rid of Chris long enough to come up with a plan.

She let out a shuddering sigh, dropping her gaze to her feet. Hoping he'd buy the submissive defeat. "I'll do it. Just don't hurt him anymore, please?" When she looked up at him, blinking, the moisture in her eyes was real. Ezra had never deserved to be caught up in her problems. And the thought of him dying… It tore her up, in ways she didn't have time to explore right now. "I just need time to regroup and figure out how to say it."

He hesitated, glancing at his watch, then back at her. "All right. Ten minutes. But that's it."

After she nodded, he strode out of the room, leaving her alone with the armed guard. The live video feed of Ezra had no sound, but she could see him crane his head toward the door of his room. Was he here, in the basement with her, only a few rooms away? Judging by the way the room looked, it made sense. And that Chris would want him close. The thought gave her a burst of hope. Maybe there was a way for them to get out of this, together.

Together.

The word stuck, and she rolled it around in her mind for a moment, like a lingering taste she didn't want to lose. But keeping him alive was far more important than dwelling on the possibility of a relationship.

Maybe she'd been going about this situation all wrong, focusing on herself the whole time. *She* needed to clear her name. *She* needed her father to know she wasn't guilty. *She* needed to do everything right to make sure she earned God's blessing.

Well, hadn't He shown her in the wilderness she didn't have to earn His blessing? That it was freely given? Couldn't He get them out of this situation if it was His will?

But maybe it *wasn't* His plan for Haley to get out. She'd never really considered the possibility before, but maybe He had some other plan she couldn't see. Maybe she wasn't supposed to take over for her father as CEO. God promised in His word that He had good plans for her, but maybe they weren't going to work out the way she'd thought.

Maybe it was time for her to step aside and let Him be in charge. Had she ever even stopped to ask what His plan for her life was? Or had she always simply plowed ahead, following everyone else's wishes and asking Him to bless her?

She took a deep breath, releasing the air slowly as she looked at Ezra's beat-up, handsome face. For a moment, he turned directly toward the camera and his clear brown eyes seemed to be staring straight at her. Almost like he wanted to say something.

Strength and warmth wrapped around her heart. She wasn't alone. God was with her, and no matter what happened, He wouldn't abandon her. That was the solution to the equation, the answer to every one of life's questions. Walking in relationship with Him.

Even if it meant sacrificing to save this man she cared about so much.

Behind her back, she uncurled her stiff fingers until her palms opened in a gesture of silent offering. The words of an old hymn drifted through her mind. *Take my life, Lord, and let it be consecrated, Lord, to Thee.*

Now to find the words to say for Chris and her father, the right words to free Ezra... But wait—

She strained forward in the chair, trying to get a better look at Ezra. He'd snapped whatever was holding his hands behind his back and was in the process of shimmying out of the ropes binding his upper body. Her breath caught as he glanced quickly over his shoulder—had the guard left his room?

Something moved in the corner of the screen. Haley gasped as camo green flashed at the edge. The guard in her room started at the sound, and she had to force herself to sigh loudly, slumping in the chair even though her heart was racing a mile a minute.

Suddenly Ezra was free. He stood, swooped up his chair and swung it at the guard in a graceful arc. Despite the lack of audio, she could almost hear the crash as the guard slumped to the floor. Would others notice?

Ezra ducked, grabbing something near the guard, before standing and darting toward the camera. He held up a finger, almost as if telling her to wait, then mouthed something. *I'm coming?*

Then his hand reached up and the screen went dark. *Lord, please keep him safe.* The prayer sprinted through her mind as she struggled to act natural. Any second now he'd be out in the hallway searching for her—the same hallway where Chris and who knew how many other armed men were waiting.

She couldn't try to loosen her own bonds, not with the guard watching, but she *could* help clear the corridor. "Okay, Chris," she called, "I'm ready."

Wait. The tablet.

Panic flared beneath her ribs. She'd forgotten about the feed going black. If Chris noticed, he'd immediately know something was wrong.

He walked in, his gaze focused on the cell phone in his hand as he tapped out some message. Every muscle stayed rigid as she watched him walk closer. Surely he'd notice that dark screen any second now.

His focus lifted from the phone, his head started to turn toward the chair—

"How are we doing this?" she asked, straining to keep her tone calm and controlled. Some of the tension in her chest leaked out as his eyes snapped to her face.

"Simple. I place a call to Ford, who puts you on speakerphone upstairs for your father to hear. We record the call in case there's any question later when we press charges. I went ahead and charged your phone for you so we can use yours." He smirked as he removed her phone from his pocket and flashed it at her.

She squeezed her fingers behind her back, gritted her teeth and nodded. "I'm ready."

"Good. What's your lock screen code?"

She told him the numbers and he placed the call, putting it on speaker so she could hear it ringing. So painful to think her father would be on the other end, wondering what was going on, waiting to hear what his only child had to say.

No sounds came from the hallway. Had Ezra gotten caught? Or had he changed his mind, realized it was smarter to get himself out and then call for backup? It might be too late for her by then, but at least he'd be safe.

"Haley, what a relief," Ford's voice came on the line in the same concerned tone he'd used when she called him from Ezra's house. A fresh sense of betrayal twisted her stomach. Who knew he was such a good actor? "Are you all right? I'm here with James," he said.

"Haley, are you there?" Her father. The words came out more uncertain, more hesitant, than she'd ever heard in her life. "Are you safe?"

A lump formed in her throat. He'd probably been worried sick over these past few days. And now, unless Ezra showed up, she was about to confess to a crime she hadn't committed and help the bad guys get his business.

Unless…she didn't. Ezra had escaped. He had a

shot at getting free. What if she warned her father instead? The worst thing they could do now was kill her. Wouldn't it be better to die honest than live a lie?

She took a deep breath, scrambling to pull together her thoughts. Chris kept his brown gaze—so cold compared to Ezra's—locked on her, as if reminding her that she needed to play along, or someone would get hurt. He waved his hand and mouthed, "Hurry up!"

Now or never.

She swallowed, but the lump didn't budge. "Hi, Dad."

Ezra paused at a junction in the hallway, his back pressed against the cold cinder-block wall. They had to be holding Haley somewhere close by—he was sure of it. Why bring him to the Whitcombe Aerotech office building, but not her?

That phone propped in his room had been connected via a Facebook Messenger call to another device. They'd been livestreaming that whole little display. He rubbed at the tender spot on his cheekbone where the guard had punched him. It had to be for Haley's benefit—otherwise, why bother bringing him here alive? No one had even asked him any questions.

All they'd done was drag him into the building, tie him up, set up the phone and turn him into a punching bag. There was only one reasonable explanation—they were using him to get to Haley. But the question was, what were they trying to get out of her?

Thankfully the phone had worked just fine to make an emergency call to Seattle PD. His precinct was in the south, but the downtown one would be pulling together a tactical team at this very moment. Backup would arrive soon.

But possibly not soon enough, especially not when Chris and Ford got wind of his escape and the missing phone. They'd know the police were coming, and he was sure they wouldn't hold back from killing anyone who stood in their way.

No, he didn't have the luxury of sitting back to wait for the police. He had to get to Haley. Now.

He dared a quick peek around the corner, then took a longer look when he didn't see anyone. This place had to be crawling with guards, but maybe they were roving the perimeter. Or all locked up with Haley. He'd taken a handgun off the man in his room and stashed it in his waistband. But the last thing he wanted to do was use it because every guard in the entire building would descend upon him in a heartbeat.

He darted down the hallway, trying to make each footfall as light and noiseless as possible. Where was she? He tugged heavy metal doors open and peeked inside, finding rooms full of mechanicals and storage, but no Haley.

Fear twisted his gut—what if he'd been wrong and she wasn't here? What if that video feed was being sent somewhere else?

Off in the distance, the rhythmic thump of footsteps echoed through the hall. Ezra ducked into the nearest room and plastered his back against the wall beside the door, holding his breath. Through the crack in the door, he watched as a man came into view—his old pal Belsky, the blond one. The man wore his typical surly expression and had his gun at the ready. He strode past Ezra's hiding place.

Ezra released a slow breath and double-checked that

the man was gone before stepping out into the hall. A short distance farther on he paused again, listening.

Voices. And one of them bore the distinct higher pitch of a woman. His heart skipped. Haley?

He tiptoed across the corridor and worked his way along the wall closer to the voices, stopping to listen at each door. Three doors down, he stilled.

Muffled words came from inside—definitely Haley. In fact, the door was slightly ajar, cracked open maybe an inch or two like whoever had entered last hadn't bothered to shut it completely. He peeked inside, but from this angle all he could see was a lone security guard.

Haley's words drifted out. "I'm really sorry, Dad. I never wanted things to end like this." The ragged edge to her voice tugged at his heart. But if she was speaking to her father, that meant either he was in the room with her, or—

"Get on with it," a man ordered in a low voice. Ford? Or perhaps that other man, Chris—the one who'd set her up in the first place? If he was busy with Haley, that left Ezra a window to take out the security guard while the other man was distracted.

He drew in a slow breath, offering a silent prayer for protection.

Then he whistled. A little trill like a mountain warbler, quiet enough he hoped only the people inside the room would hear.

They went silent. Ezra whistled again. The security guard glanced between the door and whoever else was in the room, then nodded. As he moved to open the door, Ezra flattened himself against the corridor wall.

The door opened enough to let the guard out. He

stepped into the hallway, glancing first in the opposite direction so that his back was to Ezra. Without hesitation, Ezra made his move, drawing the handgun from his waist and bringing it down hard on the back of the bigger man's head.

The man groaned as his knees gave way. Ezra caught him under the arms as he slumped to the floor and dragged him to the edge of the hall. Stashing him in another room would be the smartest thing to do, but there wasn't time. Any second whoever else was in there would realize trouble was afoot and sound the alarm.

So he left the unconscious guard slouched against the wall and pushed the door open enough to slide inside, his gun up and at the ready.

His chest ached at the sight of Haley tied up in the chair, blond hair in disarray, blue eyes glossy with tears. A man in a suit stood in front of her, holding up a cell phone—thankfully, he was the only other person in the room. He turned as soon as Ezra entered, his face whitening for an instant before the expression gave way to anger.

"How did *you* get free?" he snarled.

"Haley?" Ford Anderson's voice came through the phone he was holding, a perfectly acted tremor of fear in his tone. "What's going on? Are you okay?"

The man in the suit—who had to be Chris—swore softly under his breath and punched at the phone. With a little *bling*, the call cut out. When he started tapping again, Ezra stepped closer, keeping the gun aimed on him.

He extended his other hand. "I'll take that now, thanks."

Chris looked between him, the gun and Haley. With an impatient huff, he slapped the phone into Ezra's hand.

Ezra pointed at Haley. "Now untie her."

The other man moved painfully slowly, as if he were expecting help to arrive any second if he just stalled long enough. But as soon as he'd loosened the ropes, Haley jumped out of the chair and moved toward Ezra. He longed to tug her into an embrace, but securing Chris was first priority.

"Into the chair," he ordered, waving his gun.

"Really?" Chris looked between the two of them. "We have to do this? You're not going to get away. Ford will have texted the guards down here to check on us. I expect them to appear any second." As if to punctuate his words, footsteps thudded in the distance.

"Haley, lock that door," he said, but she was already moving. "You—get in the chair."

Chris shrugged but finally complied. As Ezra tightened the ropes around him, he said, "If you're planning on holding me hostage, or camping out in here while you wait for help, you're wasting your time. We've got all the contingencies covered."

The urge to punch him was extremely tempting, but Ezra settled for making sure the ropes were secure. He crossed the space to Haley, who was leaning against the big door.

She looked up at him, face pale, the whites showing in her eyes. "Ford is upstairs. With my father. And I can't find a lock."

"Don't worry about James, Haley." Chris smirked. "He's in good hands."

"One problem at a time." Ezra squeezed her arm, trying to reassure her. They wouldn't be foolish enough to hurt James Whitcombe, would they? Surely not. They'd never get away with it. He scanned the room, looking for anything they could use to secure the door. And an escape route. In the background, Chris laughed softly, and Ezra balled his hand into a fist.

Then his eye caught on the old furnace and duct-work. That just might work. Leaving Haley at the door, he dashed across the room to the furnace and stuffed the gun into his waistband to free his hands. The ductwork hadn't been maintained, and a three-foot-long section pried off easily with a little pressure.

"Here," he said, running back to the door. By bend-ing one end, he managed to wedge the metal beneath the lever-style door handle so that it couldn't be turned. "It won't hold them for long, though."

Chris chuckled. "And you're still trapped. I've never seen Haley so flustered. This is the best entertainment I've had in years."

Haley's lips pressed together in a thin line, her gaze darting toward Chris and then around the windowless room as her hands fluttered at her sides.

Ezra placed both hands on her cheeks, gently turning her face back toward him. Her crystal blue gaze locked on him, igniting a fire in his chest. Saving her was all that mattered right now. "Ignore him, Haley. We're get-ting out of here. Alive." He stared into her eyes, willing her to believe him. To calm down. "You can do this."

"How?"

"Through those ducts. A building this size has to have big ducts, and even if these ones aren't in use, they'll connect to the system that is."

"Okay," she breathed. Beneath his fingers, she melted into his touch. He wanted the moment to linger, but they had to go—voices rose in the corridor outside now as the guards approached the door. Reluctantly he released her, taking her arm and tugging her toward the open duct. After boosting her up, he hoisted himself into the duct after her. The thin metal creaked and shifted beneath his weight, but it held.

"Move," he told her. "They'll get into that room any second now."

Down below, someone was pounding on the metal door. Chris's voice called out, "Hurry, they're escaping into the ventilation system!"

More pounding as Haley vanished into the darkness and Ezra felt his way blindly after her. "Look for a way up," he called. "We've got to get out of here before they start firing!"

A door flew open somewhere nearby with a heavy thud. The metal ductwork made the sound disorienting. Every noise was too loud, too close.

Haley screamed as a burst of bullets tore through the thin metal ahead of her, letting in a stream of light that illuminated a halo of her loose blond hair. Another door slammed open, following seconds later by more gunfire behind Ezra.

Too late.

They were trapped.

SIXTEEN

Ezra's heart pounded like a jackhammer. There *had* to be a way out. He couldn't have led Haley up into this ventilation system to her death.

"Back up," he said, "we must've missed a connection."

She pulled close to him as another round of bullets pinged through the metal. The entire length of duct-work shook, like it might come loose from its anchors any second and send them crashing to the floor. Her breathing came in rapid gasps that tore at Ezra's heart—he'd gotten them into this situation—but she grabbed his arm.

"Look," she whispered. The bullet holes in the metal up ahead had allowed light into the otherwise pitch-dark duct, and now a junction was visible above their heads a few feet behind Ezra. They'd missed it earlier in the dark.

He scrambled backward on hands and knees. The shooting had stopped for the moment, but it would start up again as soon as the men found the room containing their section of ductwork. Then…they'd be out of time.

"You first," he told Haley, giving her space to maneuver herself upright into the duct.

"I can't find a handhold." Desperation rang in her voice. "There's no way up."

He crept closer, tapping one of her ankles. "Climb up on my back."

She hesitated, until down below, another heavy thud indicated their attackers were trying a different room. Ezra grunted as she stepped up onto his back, her boot digging painfully into his shoulder as she pushed her weight upward. Then—the strain ended as she scrambled up somewhere into the recesses of the ventilation system.

"Come on," she urged, "reach for my hands!"

Gunfire opened below, the bullets biting through the metal not two feet from where Ezra crouched. His breath froze as he struggled to get upright, squishing his shoulders into the narrow vertical duct. The metal beneath his feet swayed precariously.

Reaching up as far as he could, he groped in the darkness for Haley's hands until his fingers brushed against hers. He'd have to jump to get a good grip, but in this enclosed space, with the metal breaking below…

Maybe he could wedge himself into the vertical duct instead. Pressing his back against one of the sides, he braced his hands against the opposite wall and lifted his feet. None too soon because another round of bullets ripped through the metal he'd just left. By God's grace the angle sent them tearing through the duct below him, but all it would take was somebody standing directly beneath him and he'd be toast.

He pushed upward, sliding his back up the metal, then stopping to brace himself again. A few feet were enough to bring his hands into easy contact with Haley's. She slipped her fingers around his, tugging him up and into the next horizontal duct.

The section of ductwork they'd just abandoned groaned ominously, and with a loud crash, tore loose and plunged to the floor. Random shots bit into the ceiling below them, punctuated by intermittent cursing, and light rushed up through the vertical duct they'd climbed.

"Go," Ezra whispered, waiting as Haley struggled to turn herself around in the narrow space. Then he followed her, hands and knees thumping lightly on the metal.

The shots tapered off as they crawled deeper into the duct, pushing farther in and upward at every opportunity, trying to get clear of the basement sublevels. Finally, they reached a part of the system in use, as evidenced by the intermittent blasts of cold air rushing past.

After a long time, Haley paused and looked back at him over her shoulder. "We need to get to the tenth floor. That's where Ford has my father."

"Agreed. I called Seattle PD downstairs before I found you, but it'll take them a while to get a SWAT team into the building."

"Ezra…" Her voice broke. "Won't the police make them even more desperate?"

"We'll get to him in time." He squeezed her ankle reassuringly. "But we need to get out of the ventilation system to move faster."

She crawled on in silence for a few more minutes, then paused as they approached a junction through which faint light diffused into the duct. "There." She pointed to a vent cover.

"Let me check it out." Ezra wedged past her, pressing

his face close to the cover. They'd passed a few already that led into individual offices and were too narrow to squeeze through, but this one looked like an intake and had a larger panel. Through the slits he could just make out a large conference room, lit only by the dim orange safety lighting for night. The last time he'd checked a phone, it'd read 10:17 p.m. Late.

The panel clanged softly as he pushed it out of place and set it aside on the floor. After crawling out onto the carpeted floor, he helped Haley as she emerged after him. His stiff muscles rejoiced at the chance to stretch after being cooped up in the ducts. But they needed to get moving—it wouldn't take the men below long to figure out where they were heading.

"Emergency stairs are this way," Haley urged, taking his hand and pulling him into the hallway. "Looks like we're on—" she glanced at the room numbers as they raced toward one end "—the second floor. Come on!"

They made it to the emergency staircase at the end of the hall unhindered, then took the stairs up two at a time. His legs burned and his lungs ached as they passed one floor after another. Far below, a door banged open and he jerked to a halt, grabbing Haley.

Together they froze, backs against the cinder-block wall, chests heaving as they sucked in great gasps of air. Footsteps pounded up the staircase several floors down until another door slammed open. When the stairwell grew silent, they kept running.

Finally, a large number ten painted on the wall in block print announced they'd reached the right floor. Haley punched the security code into a small keypad beside the door and, with a click, the lock opened. The floor was eerily silent as Ezra followed her through the doorway and into the softly padded hallway full of dark offices and closed doors.

Light streamed in a long rectangle from one open doorway far down the long corridor. Haley paused, glancing back at him, her face glowing orange in the building's dim night lighting. Low, indistinguishable male voices drifted toward them.

"Maybe I should go first," she whispered. "Try to get a confession. You can record it on the phone you took from Chris."

He chewed the inside of his cheek, looking both ways up and down the empty hall. From what he could see, there weren't any guards up here—maybe all part of Ford's ruse that everything was as it should be—but he still hated the idea of sending Haley in to confront Ford alone. The man had already betrayed her. Who knew how far he would stoop?

"Please, Ezra. He's such a good actor, and without a confession... I'm afraid a jury will never convict him." Haley's soft words brought his attention back to her face. Creases lined her forehead and dark circles lingered beneath her eyes, a constant reminder of the trauma she'd endured over the past week. He took her face in his hands, his thumb rubbing against her soft cheek as if he could wipe away what she'd gone through. But this was her battle, and unless her life was directly in danger, she should get to decide how things played out.

"Okay. But first sign of trouble, I'm coming in. Deal?"

"Yeah," she breathed. For a fleeting moment the world disappeared and all he could see were Haley's gorgeous, trusting eyes staring up at him. Impulse took over and he pulled her closer until his lips pressed against hers for one glorious, breath-stealing second.

Then he released her, his heart already twisting with the pain of the goodbye that was coming. *If* they got out of this situation intact. "See you soon."

Her throat bobbed and she nodded. He trailed a few paces behind her as she approached the open door.

With a silent prayer, he watched her step into the room.

Haley blinked at the bright floodlighting in the conference room. Whether intentionally or not, Ford had chosen the same space where she'd caught Chris photographing the plans. Only a few days ago, and yet it felt like a lifetime.

Ford scowled and her father looked up in surprise as she stopped inside the doorway, her back braced against the wall to support her suddenly sagging knees. Papers were spread out on the table between them, along with a pen and a cell phone. Her father's face bore traces of fatigue and confusion, but despite the circumstances he still held himself with his typical confidence. Like someone scheming to steal your business was an everyday occurrence.

Ford broke the silence first. "Haley, what a…surprise. We didn't expect you to come confess in person." He glanced toward the dark doorway behind her. "Are you alone?"

No, thankfully, she wasn't. Just thinking about Ezra filled her entire being with warmth. But this wasn't his problem, and she needed him to escape this situation alive.

She leveled a glare at Ford, mustering all the confidence she could cobble together. "I didn't come here to confess. But perhaps you'd like a chance, before the police arrive?"

"Haley?" James's deep bass echoed through the silent room as he glanced between her and Ford. "What's going on here? Where have you been?"

"I caught Chris photographing the plans, Dad, after he killed the security guard."

"But the murder weapon was found in *your* office, Haley." Ford enunciated each word like he was talking to a three-year-old. He shrugged helplessly at her father, as if there could be no question about her guilt, and she was the one living in denial. "Why are you trying to blame Chris?"

Frustration burned the back of her throat at the confused look on James's face. "He planted it after I escaped. Who would be foolish enough to stash a murder weapon in their own office? Besides, I've got the proof."

Well, she *had* the proof. Now Ford had it—unless he'd wiped the flash drive already. Something flickered across his face and his hand drifted toward his jacket, then stopped. Like he'd forgotten about it.

Maybe there was still a chance.

She plowed on, telling her father the whole story. "He intended to sell the plans to that Swiss company you turned down last year, but when he saw me, he sent men to kill me and retrieve the evidence. They chased me until my plane went down in North Cascades National Park. A ranger helped me get back to Ford." Her voice caught on the word *ranger*, but she kept going. "But Ford betrayed me and brought me back here to extort a confession. I'm still not sure why you didn't just kill us out there."

James Whitcombe pulled back, staring at him. "*Ford?* How could you?"

He believed her. Hope flooded her chest.

Ford's face drained of color and emotions warred across his features. Then he stiffened, his expression hardening. "Well, I guess we don't really have time to keep up this little ruse any longer, do we? James, you should've listened to me when you had the chance. That deal would've propelled me into the upper echelons of corporate law. But you never thought about anyone else, did you?

"As for you, Haley, once you spilled your little story to that innocent ranger and dragged him into it, we had to clean up the mess. Once you got in touch with me, it made more sense to let you get to me, where I could bring you in to make your confession, than resort to cold-blooded killing that might arouse suspicions."

Her eyebrows lifted as realization dawned. "They *let* us escape. On the trail to Stehekin when we were coming to meet you…"

A humorless smile twisted his lips. "Not exactly. They were supposed to escort you to the airstrip. But once you'd gotten loose, it made more sense to let you go, since you were coming to me anyway. Capturing the ranger was necessary to make sure he didn't tell anyone else. And for insurance." A wicked gleam lit up his eyes. "Now though, we've chatted long enough. Time to sign the papers."

"I don't think so." She pulled back, bumping against the wall. "A SWAT team is on the way—might be out front this very minute."

Her father's steady blue gaze found hers for the first time, and she could feel his love and strength in that one look. He turned to Ford. "We would never sign this business over to someone like Chris." His voice dropped lower. "I'm disappointed, Ford. You were my friend. Chris, though—I had a hunch he wasn't the right fit for Whitcombe Aerotech."

"Sorry to let you down, old friend—" Ford offered a phony smile "—but I've had to take matters into my hands. Legal counsel isn't as lucrative a career as one might think, and I've got to plan for my future."

"In jail?" Haley snapped.

"Hardly." Ford reached beneath the table, and when he withdrew his hand, the shiny metal surface of a gun gleamed in the bright overhead lighting. James drew back, his fingers going to his open mouth in horrified shock as Ford released the safety and swiveled the gun to aim at him.

Panic flared beneath Haley's ribs, squeezing her chest in a painful grip.

He went on, "Now, all you need to do is sign the papers, clear up this little…*misunderstanding*…with the police, and we'll all be on our merry way."

"Or what?" her father demanded. "You'll shoot us and go to jail?"

"No. I'll shoot you, James, and then barely escape with my life, perhaps with a gunshot wound to the leg—" he shrugged "—and Haley will go to jail. If she doesn't decide to kill herself first. Conveniently, the will you signed five years ago states that I, as your trusted friend and attorney, will assume full control of Whitcombe Aerotech in the event of both your and Haley's… incapacitation. Since we both agreed I'd do a better job managing your interests than dear old Aunt Lissy. Who are the police going to believe? An upstanding citizen like me, or a woman wanted for murder?"

Motion blurred in the doorway as Ezra stepped in, his handgun up and trained on Ford. "Lower the weapon, Mr. Anderson. I'm placing you under arrest."

"Arrest?" Ford snarled, his eyes darting from her father to Ezra. "Aren't you a park ranger?"

"Yes, but I'm an officer with the Seattle PD the rest of the year. I can assure you a SWAT team is on the way, so put the gun down and place your hands on your head."

"Actually—" Ford lifted the gun to James's head "—you'd better lower yours before someone gets hurt."

"You know I can't do that." Ezra's voice carried a hint of steel beneath the calm.

Stalemate. Haley's chest was so tight she could hardly breathe. "It's too late, Ford," she insisted, trying to keep the desperation from leaking into her voice. "The police will find Chris and all those hired gunmen and my name will be cleared. Ezra, did you record his confession?"

"You know it," Ezra replied.

Red crept up Ford's neck, but his expression remained complacent. "Nothing I can't delete. Maybe Chris *is* behind all of this. He locked us up in this room together. Since Haley and her corrupt park ranger friend are working with him, they turned on us."

Ezra didn't flinch. "Even if you kill James, you won't live long enough to blame us for it."

"The point is, nobody has to die," Ford said. "All James has to do is sign. Or we could keep waiting to see who gets here first—the police, or backup from the basement. I'm willing to wager it'll be Chris's men."

The room was so silent, Haley could hear every one of her father's ragged gasps. She tucked her trembling hands into balls at her side.

Her father reached for the pen on the table, his fingers shaking.

"Don't do it, Mr. Whitcombe." A muscle worked in Ezra's jaw, and his knuckles were white around the upraised gun.

Ford's lips curled. "Isn't this a fun little dilemma? You can't shoot me when I have Mr. Whitcombe at point-blank range. But you know I can't sit here all day, waiting around to get arrested. Thirty seconds should be enough time to sign. That's reasonable, don't you think?"

"Dad, you've invested your entire life in this company." Tears blurred Haley's vision, and she blinked them impatiently away.

James took a steadying breath. His eyes met hers "I'm sorry, Haley, but we've got to try. *You've* always been the most important part of my life."

Emotions battled within her chest—pride at her father's words and the love in his eyes, fear over what might happen. She glanced at Ezra. Though he stood still as a statue, his gaze fixed on Ford, he slowly pried the thumb of his supporting hand away from his other wrist and waved it toward the doorway behind them, like he was trying to tell her something. But what?

Surely he didn't expect her to run?

Then his gaze flicked up to the ceiling, so briefly she almost didn't catch the motion. She followed the track his eyes had taken, and then she saw it.

The sprinkler.

He wanted her to pull the fire alarm.

Her back was already against the doorjamb. She only had to slide a few inches closer to Ezra, angle her body just so—and wedge her arm out between her side and the doorjamb. As she moved closer to the door, Ezra moved too, sliding forward one slow inch at a time to keep Ford from noticing.

Sometime in the span of the last few seconds, her father had clicked on the pen and was slowly scrawling his signature across the page. Ford stared at the motion. They were almost out of time.

Giving up on stealth, she groped blindly for the fire alarm. Funny how a thing she'd ignored for so many years was now the one thing she needed desperately to find. Finally her fingers brushed against the plastic case. She flipped it up, yanking on the metal pull just as Ford realized she'd moved.

"Hey—"

His voice cut off as the high-pitched alarm shrieked from the speakers overhead and emergency lighting flashed. Startled, Ford glanced up at the ceiling, his eyes wide and jaw slack in the pulsating white lights. The gun drooped in his hands.

Ezra seized the moment of distraction instantly, lunging across the table and knocking the gun out of Ford's hand as he took the older man to the floor.

"Dad, get out of there!" Haley urged, waving her father toward her.

He rolled his chair away from Ezra and Ford, spun around and rushed on wobbling legs around the conference table. Haley took his arm and practically shoved him out into the hallway. Her blood froze as the door to the emergency stairs at the far end of the hall flung open.

But instead of men in fatigues with AK-47s, an

army of officers clad in black vests and helmets poured through the door. The SWAT team.

Relief made her knees go weak until the sharp crack of a gunshot resounded through the small conference room she'd just left.

"Ezra!" She ducked her head around the doorjamb to see inside the room. The space had gone deathly silent. Her heart catapulted into her throat and she bent low, searching beneath the table for any sign of motion on the other side.

Nothing. Just four legs clearly visible lying on the carpet.

Maybe Ford had won and come away with the gun, but it was a risk she'd take. Stumbling inside, she rushed around the table, leaping over a gun. Ezra lay on his back, the second gun a foot away from his outstretched hand. On his other side, Ford groaned and struggled to rise, then gave up and fell back onto his face.

"Ezra?" She dropped to her knees next to him, placing both hands on his chest. Feeling for any sign of obvious injury. But her hands came away dry, and his heart thumped steadily beneath her fingers.

He reached up a hand to brush her cheek. "Haley? Are you all right?"

A wave of relief threatened to crush her. "I thought… I heard the shot and…"

"*I'm* the one who got shot," Ford moaned, still managing to sound indignant. "In the leg."

"It was your own fault." Ezra pulled himself up into a sitting position as members of the SWAT team rushed into the room. A flashlight shone in their faces, blinding them for a moment.

"Ezra Dalton?" one of the officers asked, dropping the light to their feet.

"Watkins, is that you?" A crooked smile lit up his face.

The other man stepped around Ford and shook Ezra's hand. "Hey, man, you all right?"

"We are now that you're here. This one—" he jerked his head toward Ford "—needs to be locked up. Did you get the men in the basement?"

"A whole string of them, down in the garage trying to evac."

Thank You, God. They were safe. Her fingers found Ezra's and interlaced. He turned to look at her. "How's your father?"

"Safe, thanks to you." Pressure built in her chest, threatening to squeeze out her eyes as tears. "Along with his company. I don't know how to thank you for what you did."

"I didn't do it alone. You're a truly remarkable woman, Haley." When he leaned down, his warm brown eyes fixed on her face, stretching up to kiss him was the most natural thing in the world.

She could've kept sitting there forever, so wrapped up in that moment with Ezra that the whole world had faded away and she didn't even notice the blaring siren, but the police officers were ready to help them to their feet.

Right. Technically, she was still a wanted criminal. And Ezra had been abducted from the national park without ever having the chance to talk to his employer. Plus the Callahans must be worried sick about them. *And* their horses.

She squeezed his hand one last time. Letting go hurt,

like she was a piece of fabric being ripped in two. But right now, there were too many things they had to resolve. Possibly too many things for a relationship to ever work. Maybe these intense feelings would fade with time, and they'd each move on with their lives as if nothing had changed.

Her heart hurt as the police led her and her father toward the emergency stairs. She turned back at the doorway, and Ezra lifted a hand in farewell.

Biting back tears, she stumbled through the exit after her father and back to the life she'd always thought she wanted.

SEVENTEEN

Haley's finger hovered over the computer mouse. She drew in a steadying breath, offered a silent prayer and clicked "submit."

A moment later, a message popped up on the screen. *Thank you for applying to the University of Washington's graduate degree program in engineering.*

She leaned back in her chair, her heart lighter than it had been in months. Years, actually.

The last month since that traumatic night at Whitcombe Aerotech had sped by in a blur. Between the memory stick the police recovered from Ford, her and her father's accounts and the testimony Ezra gave remotely by Zoom call, her name had been cleared. Now Ford Anderson, Chris Collins and their hired men were locked away in jail, awaiting trial, while the FBI worked to track down their international buyer.

After they'd gotten through the legal process of clearing her name, her father had called her into his office.

"Haley," he'd asked, "I never once even stopped to consider if you want to take over my business. I'm sorry I never thought to ask. Is this what you want?"

For one brief moment, the old Haley had wanted to say, "Yes, of course!" Anything to make him happy.

But she couldn't, not now that she knew what it was doing to her soul. How she'd lost herself over all these years, striving to be somebody she wasn't, and ignored the Lord's gentle nudging to use the gifts He'd given her.

So she'd shaken her head. "No, Dad, it isn't." She'd braced herself for his reaction.

But he'd merely lifted an eyebrow. "I thought so. What *do* you want?"

"I want to work for R&D as a project manager. I want to invent stuff." It sounded silly, but the thought of getting to do what she wanted… It made her feel like she was floating.

With her father's blessing, she'd thrown herself headlong into studying for and taking her GRE exam, gathering her transcripts, requesting letters of recommendation and writing essays. All for this moment.

And it felt good. But the trouble was, a giant piece of her heart was still missing, and she knew exactly where to find it.

Out in North Cascades National Park, with Ezra Dalton. Time and distance had done nothing to erase the deep connection they'd forged, and as excited as she was about the possibility of the new life before her, it wouldn't mean anything without him.

As she stared at the message on her laptop, she prayed. *Lord, is now the right time?*

Peace flooded her heart, the kind that defied human understanding. Maybe Ezra wasn't interested, maybe he didn't feel the same way she did, but she had to try. Had to tell him how much she loved him.

She shot off a quick text to her father. Application submitted to UW.

His reply came back immediately. Congrats! Want the plane to celebrate? I hear the North Cascades are pretty.

A smile played on her lips. She'd explained everything that Ezra had done for her, but she'd been careful to barely mention him since then. Apparently, she hadn't been as careful as she'd thought.

Thanks. Love you.

Her fingers hesitated over the email app. She'd only heard from Ezra once in the past month—a short message letting her know he'd cleared everything up with his boss, they'd found the Callahans' horses, and he'd be appearing in court to testify against Ford and Chris. His email had come in the midst of sorting through everything with the lawyers, and though she'd longed to send back a lengthy response, she'd kept her reply as brief and on-task as his had been.

Did it mean he wasn't interested? That he'd forgotten her, or moved on with his life?

She swallowed. There was only one way to find out, and if she didn't seize her chance, she'd regret it the rest of her life.

Her message was brief. I know it's last minute, but I'm flying into Stehekin tonight and staying at the lodge for a week. Needed some down time. If you get this, and you want to see me, you know where to find me.

The plane jolted to a stop after a bumpy landing on the grassy Stehekin airstrip. Haley opened the door, taking a deep breath of the fresh mountain air. The sky was bright blue, glistening with promise as fluffy white clouds danced across the jagged mountain peaks surrounding the valley.

It was the kind of day where anything felt possible.

She grabbed her overnight bag out of the cockpit, secured the plane and strode over the mown grass to the dirt road. A month had passed since the last time she'd been here, and yet it felt like a lifetime. She was a different person now, but was Ezra? He hadn't responded to her email, though for all she knew he was out on the trail. But still the doubts nagged her—what if he didn't come? What if he wasn't ready to consider a relationship, or didn't feel the same way?

Hopeful nerves fluttered in her stomach anyway as she caught the bus into the tiny town and checked into her room.

The next morning, over breakfast, she reminded herself that the earliest he could possibly arrive was probably later that day. Even if he'd left his house the second he got her email, he still had to either ride in on horseback or navigate his way to Chelan and take the ferry.

There was no reason to worry.

But as the days wore on with no word from him, doubts assailed her. Haley passed the time wandering around the grounds, going on a trail ride, and sitting on the lodge's porch sipping iced tea. She couldn't bring herself to visit the bakery or sit on the dock where she'd sat with him before.

Maybe he didn't *want* to see her.

The final morning arrived. She could stall a little longer. Her father didn't expect her to return until evening. Maybe it was time to ask about him, just to see if he'd had a chance to even read her email. With her bag slung over her shoulder, she traipsed down the wooded road to the ranger station. The uniformed man behind the desk looked young enough to be in high school, but she guessed he was probably a college student.

"Excuse me, but can you tell me where Ezra Dalton is assigned right now? He's a backcountry ranger here."

The kid pulled out a printed list and double-checked the dates against his calendar. "He's on a six-day patrol. Scheduled to get home today."

Her heart sank. He'd headed out the day after she sent the email. Maybe he'd missed reading it before he left.

Or decided not to respond until after his patrol. Wouldn't that be the easiest way to let her down?

Sorry, I missed your message. Maybe it'll work out next time.

"Okay, thanks."

She gathered her bag off the floor and trudged the long, dusty miles back to the airstrip. Walking didn't really help the pain squeezing her heart, but somehow it seemed easier than taking the bus.

As she approached the plane, she let her gaze wander across the mountains surrounding the valley. This would probably be her last visit out here. The thought stuck in her throat, making it hard to swallow.

But when she reached the plane, she stopped short. Blinked. Was that…

Ezra?

Ezra stood next to the pilot's side, one arm casually propped up on the wing like waiting for the woman he loved was an everyday occurrence. He'd unloaded his heavy backpack onto the ground nearby, and he ran a hand through his mussy hair as movement flickered through the trees on the path leading to the airstrip.

Then she was there—blond hair blowing in the wind, cheeks pink with exertion, blue eyes widening as she finally noticed him. Even more beautiful than his memory had made her. His heart stuttered as she dropped her bag and flung herself toward him.

He caught her in his arms and she buried her face in his shoulder, sobbing into his shirt, the fabric balled up beneath her fingers. Holding her again, being the one to comfort her and keep her safe—it felt like the most natural thing in the world. Like finally coming home.

"Shhh," he whispered, rubbing his hand on her back. He pressed the other against her head, his fingers in her soft hair. "It's okay, Haley. I've got you."

Finally, she pulled back, swiping at her cheeks and turning her face down, as if she wanted to hide.

He tilted her chin back up and brushed a tear away from her cheek. "I missed you. So much, it's been killing me."

Haley's whole face brightened, like she'd been worried he didn't care. "I missed you too," she said. "There are so many things I've wanted to tell you. I emailed last week before I came out here, but maybe you didn't get it. Which reminds me—aren't you supposed to be on patrol?"

"Yeah, about that…" He laughed. "Our internet was out before I left so I couldn't check email, but apparently a few days ago this bigwig CEO called headquarters to talk to my boss, who then called me on the radio and said I was needed at Stehekin Airport just as soon as I could get in here." He glanced at his watch. "Which was about twenty minutes ago."

Her cheeks glowed. "My dad told you I was coming?"

He grinned like a kid at Christmas, remembering that message coming through on his radio. Haley had flown in, just to see him. If he'd entertained any doubts about his feelings, they'd evaporated at that moment. "You can believe that was the fastest I've ever hiked in my life."

So much had happened in his heart since that painful day they'd had to separate in Seattle, when he'd realized exactly how deeply he'd fallen in love with Haley and how much it hurt to be apart from her. A different kind of raw, aching loss than he'd felt after Sarah's death, but just as painful. In these last few weeks, God had been at work, gently teaching, mending, nudging him onward in faith. It was time to offer that newly healed heart back to Haley. From the way she'd sobbed into his shirt, he had a pretty good idea the feelings were mutual.

He took her hands in his. "After I lost my wife and daughter, I never thought I'd feel that way about anyone ever again. Then you came along, totally different than Sarah, this whirlwind of life and energy—" his heart swelled as he soaked in every inch of her face "—and I fell in love with you. It terrified me. I felt like I was betraying Sarah's memory. But then I realized, she wouldn't want me to live stuck in the past. She would've wanted God to heal my heart and let me find love again. To be happy. The same thing I would've wanted for her. She and Kaitlyn will always have a place in my heart, but—" he blinked away the tears pushing into his eyes "—this month away from you has been torture. I can't imagine facing the rest of my life without you."

Her lips parted, eyes glowing softly under a sheen of moisture. "I've been lost in my work for so long, and in this effort to impress everyone around me. Unwilling to admit my loneliness or trust myself in another relationship after my horrible breakup. But for the first time, with you, I saw how pointless all my striving was and how someone could love me for just who I am. You challenged me to be the best version of my true self. You make me come alive, Ezra."

How was it possible to bind so much happiness up into one heart? Especially when he thought he'd never feel this way again? God was so good.

A question was burning its way through his insides, and the time had come to ask it. His lips tilted at the way Haley's eyes widened as he dropped down onto one knee. "Haley Whitcombe, you are God's gift in my life, and I never want to be apart from you again. I know there's no jumbotron, but will you—"

"Yes!" She pried one hand out of his to wipe her cheeks, then pulled him to his feet. "One hundred percent yes. I'm so in love with you, Ezra Dalton, I didn't know I could hold this many feelings."

"You didn't even let me finish the question." Typical Haley. His lips twitched as joy bubbled up inside.

"Yes, I will marry you. I applied to graduate school for a Master's degree in engineering, so if I get in I'll have to be in class most of the year, but we can live out here in the summer if you want. Or stay in Seattle. I don't care. As long as I'm with you."

"No CEO?" He glanced around at the pristine wilderness surrounding them. "Though I'd miss it, I'd give this up for you."

"No CEO. That's not who God made me to be, not really." She drew in a deep breath. "I'm just a girl who wants to design cool stuff and get lost in the woods with her handsome park ranger husband."

He leaned closer, until his face was only inches from hers. "Now that's a plan I can get on board with."

Their lips pressed together in a kiss, the first of many in a lifetime of love and adventure.

* * * * *

*If you enjoyed this story,
don't miss Kellie VanHorn's
next thrilling romantic suspense,
available next year from
Love Inspired Suspense!*

*Find more great reads at
www.LoveInspired.com*

Dear Reader,

Thank you so much for hitting the trail with Ezra and Haley! I've never been backpacking myself, but I had a blast imagining their wilderness adventure. To plan their route, I ordered a topographic map of North Cascades National Park online. One of my teenage sons spent hours poring over the map with me, and now he has big plans for us to go backpacking in the Cascades.

Both Ezra and Haley wrestle with why God allows bad things to happen in our lives. Deep down, Ezra wonders if he can truly trust God or if he has to protect his own heart. Haley thinks she must earn God's favor. They both come to learn that while we can't avoid the trials of life, God offers us the ultimate gift—Himself—and we'll never have to face the hard things alone. May we find our hope and joy in that comfort!

I love hearing from readers, so feel free to get in touch on Facebook (Author Kellie VanHorn) or through my website www.kellievanhorn.com, where you can sign up for my newsletter.

Warm regards,
Kellie VanHorn

LOVE INSPIRED

Stories to uplift and inspire

Fall in love with Love Inspired—
inspirational and uplifting stories of faith
and hope. Find strength and comfort in
the bonds of friendship and community.
Revel in the warmth of possibility and the
promise of new beginnings.

Sign up for the Love Inspired newsletter
at **LoveInspired.com** to be the first
to find out about upcoming titles,
special promotions and exclusive content.

CONNECT WITH US AT:

Facebook.com/LoveInspiredBooks

Twitter.com/LoveInspiredBks

LISOCIAL2021

COMING NEXT MONTH FROM
Love Inspired Suspense

DEFENDING FROM DANGER
Rocky Mountain K-9 Unit • by Jodie Bailey
Multiple attacks aren't enough to scare off wolf sanctuary owner
Paige Bristow—especially once she calls in her ex, K-9 officer
Reece Campbell, and his partner, Maverick, for protection. But will a
secret connection between Reece and Paige's daughter threaten their
attempt to stop the danger from escalating into something lethal?

TEXAS BURIED SECRETS
Cowboy Lawmen • by Virginia Vaughan
Publicly vowing to bring a serial killer to justice, Deputy Cecile Richardson
solidifies herself as the criminal's next target. Can Sheriff Josh Avery keep
her safe long enough to identify and catch the culprit—or will the killer
successfully hunt down his prey?

CAVERN COVER-UP
by Katy Lee
Suspecting her father's murder is linked to a smuggling ring sends private
investigator Danika Lewis pursuing a lead all the way to Carlsbad Caverns
National Park. Teaming up with ranger Tru Butler to search the caves for the
missing artifacts is the fastest way to uncover the truth that a killer will do
anything to keep hidden.

SABOTAGED MISSION
by Tina Radcliffe
When an investigation leaves CIA operative Mackenzie "Mac" Sharp injured
and her partner presumed dead, Mac must hide to survive. But her fellow
operative and ex-boyfriend, Gabe Denton, tracks her down—leading a well-
connected enemy straight to her. Now with someone trying to frame and kill
her, Gabe's the only person she can trust.

SHIELDING THE TINY TARGET
by Deena Alexander
Accepting help from Jack Moretta is widow Ava Colburn's last chance after
her late husband's killers track her down and target her little girl. Ava's been
running from these murderers for years, and Jack could be just what this
family needs to put the deadly past behind them once and for all...

HIDDEN RANCH PERIL
by Michelle Aleckson
After witnessing her aunt's abduction, veterinarian Talia Knowles will do
anything to find her—even as the kidnappers set their sights on her. Could
relying on neighboring ranch hand Noah Landers be the key to finding her
aunt and discovering the culprits' true motives?

**LOOK FOR THESE AND OTHER LOVE INSPIRED BOOKS WHEREVER
BOOKS ARE SOLD, INCLUDING MOST BOOKSTORES, SUPERMARKETS,
DISCOUNT STORES AND DRUGSTORES.**

LISCNM0622

Get 4 FREE REWARDS!

We'll send you 2 FREE Books plus 2 FREE Mystery Gifts.

FREE
Value Over
$20

Both the **Love Inspired®** and **Love Inspired®** Suspense series feature compelling novels filled with inspirational romance, faith, forgiveness, and hope.

SPECIAL EXCERPT FROM

LOVE INSPIRED SUSPENSE
INSPIRATIONAL ROMANCE

Publicly vowing to bring a serial killer to justice, Deputy Cecile Richardson solidifies herself as the criminal's next target. Can Sheriff Josh Avery keep her safe long enough to identify and catch the culprit—or will Cecile become the killer's next victim?

Read on for a sneak peek at
Texas Buried Secrets *by Virginia Vaughan!*

Within ten minutes of her call, Cecile's home and property were surrounded by sheriff's deputies and forensics personnel.

Josh was one of the first to arrive. He found her on the couch. He'd never seen her look so fragile before. It worried him—even though her demeanor changed the moment she saw him. She slipped on her mask of confidence as she stood to face him.

"What happened?" He resisted the urge to pull her into an embrace. Not only would that be unprofessional, but he didn't want to blur the lines between them any more than they already were.

"A man broke into my house." She explained hearing the glass breaking and then finding the broken glass and dirty shoe print. "He grabbed me from behind and knocked my gun out of my hands, but I managed to fight him off."

Josh glanced at the trail of blood. She'd connected with the assailant.

"I elbowed him. Think I broke his nose. He ran after that—didn't even take his stuff with him." She gestured over to the counter.

As proud as he was that she'd successfully defended herself, the pride didn't ease his panic at the sight of the shower curtain and clothesline. She could take care of herself, but that didn't make it any easier to accept that she'd been targeted. He didn't know if this had anything to do with the case—but the shower curtain and line the assailant left behind suggested it did. They might have just caught a break, but at what expense? He wouldn't risk Cecile's life even to catch a serial killer.

She rubbed her arms and he spotted goose bumps on them. "I'd better go clean up before someone sees me like this."

She walked across the hall into the bathroom and shut the door. He checked the rest of the windows and then double-checked the locks. The house was as secure as he could make it for now—but that wasn't nearly as secure as he'd like.

The presence of the shower curtain and clothesline seemed to suggest she'd been deliberately targeted. Josh prayed the blood evidence would provide them with a DNA match, but that would be days, maybe weeks, away. They couldn't wait that long. He'd already lost Haley to a killer.

He couldn't lose Cecile, too.

Don't miss
Texas Buried Secrets *by Virginia Vaughan,*
available August 2022 wherever
Love Inspired Suspense books and ebooks are sold.

LoveInspired.com

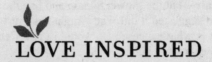